FORGIVE & FORGET ME NOT

A True Story

Joe Forte

Xulon Press
www.xulonpress.com

To order additional copies, call 1-866-909-BOOK (2665).

DEDICATED TO THE
LOVING MEMORY OF

*Michelle
Lentine-Forte*

I WILL NEVER FORGET YOU.

Special thanks to those who have touched my life over the last ten years. Thank you Lord God and my Savior Jesus Christ for saving me from myself, and giving me hope for this life and the life yet to come. My dear sweet wife Rachel, for standing by my side, not giving up on me and for seeing something in me that I could not see for myself. To my wonderful parents, Joe and Rosalie Forte, who with their love and support made this book possible. Thank you to my sister Theresa and my brother-in-law Michael Smith, Natalie & Larry Willoughby, Rita & John Donaldson, Mary & Jim Jones, Michael, Nicholas, Frank, Anthony, and Rick & Michelle Greenblatt. My loving Grandparents Josephine Forte, Anna Monteleone and Giuseppe Monteleone. Brenda Aldridge, John Richards, and the Warnock Family. My church families and the pastors of Hope Baptist Church in Las Vegas, Nevada and First Baptist Church Woodstock, in Woodstock, Georgia. The Monroe County District Attorney's office, the Department of Victims & Witness Assistance, the entire Greece Police Department, and the Community of Rochester, New York. FedEx and my managers and coworkers wherever you all may be. May God's blessings be on each and every one of you wherever you are.

FOREWORD

I know I have put this off for long enough. There is a good possibility the main reason is, part of me is still afraid to let out all the bad feelings again by going through the memories. Another part of me understands that writing all this down is essential to bringing closure to the chapter in my life that changed my views on everything forever.

My first attempt was the fall of 1994, a mere eighteen months after my wife Michelle was murdered when I wrote a paper for my English class. The feelings were still a little too close to home for me then. I would no longer cry when I told my story, but instead my heart would race in my chest and my hands would shake, as the anger and bitterness inside me would rise up again. There were times during that paper that I felt like I was going to explode with anger, but thank God my rational side would take control at those moments.

Now more than eight years have gone by, and the more time goes by, the bigger the picture gets. I continue to gain a better understanding of how much Michelle's life and death have changed me and rearranged my priorities in life. I guess that's what wisdom is, learning from your past and growing from your experiences, and understanding the broad array of past circumstances and how they fit into your life today.

I am not the same person I was nine years ago. Tragedy tends to age you, but most of all if it is handled in the correct way it can also help you to grow emotionally and spiritually. I don't believe it is wise to live in the past, or let your past adversely effect or disable you from doing your best to live the one life that God has so generously given us. However, it is very important to gain perspective from our past and use it to effectively minister and counsel others.

The main reason the Bible focuses so much on the struggles and hardships of God's people is because from their lives we may gain the knowledge that, with faith in God, we may achieve peace and victory.

Since Michelle's death, I have returned to college and graduated, gotten re-married to a wonderful and supportive woman, and become a father to two beautiful and intelligent daughters who are the absolute joy of my life. Even though I feel time has done a great bit to ease my pain, it has been the love and support of my family and friends, and my close relationship with my savior Jesus that has helped me through the rough times. I still tend to get worked up when I think or talk about it, but sometimes I still can't believe this tragedy was part of my life. I understand this is all part of the healing and growth process though. I guess people knew what they where talking about when they said, " the pain will never really fully go away, but we can learn to use it in a positive way".

Besides the stirred up emotions talking about this may bring, a second reason I have put it off so long is that I feel my life is still a work in progress. Believe me this would have been a much different book had I written it say four or five years ago. I am developing a much different perspective and greater understanding as time goes on. Further, I do not want to exploit what happened for pure shock value in order to entertain people, but I feel it is very important to the message that I am trying to get across that I do cover the details of Michelle's life and her murder so you can have a better understanding of where I am coming from and just how awful a situation this truly was. I hope to find a midway point between simply just telling a tragic story, and using the lessons that I have learned to help others who suffer loss. This story has to be told in this manner, especially in the wake of our country's recent epidemic of growing violence. I can tell you first hand what a family goes through when senseless violence touches close to home. An underlying theme of this book however, is a story of triumph over tragedy, and the important lessons I have learned which have helped me grow into a stronger person who is more in touch than I ever was before.

I wanted to do something with my life that would clearly show I have over come this tragedy and really moved on with my life.

Maybe just writing this book is all that I'm supposed to do, or it may well be that the book is the way I reach the people I want to help. Whatever it is that I'm supposed to do later on in life, I do know today God is pushing me towards telling my story, and who am I to doubt him. Believe me I have put up many objections to completing this process, but there has always been that feeling deep down in my soul that there is something I have yet to complete. The problem is the feeling would just not go away.

This in no way can be considered an autobiography, because frankly I haven't lived long enough or done anything of great social significance at this point in my life. If nothing else this story is a fulfillment of a promise I made to Michelle after she died, and I don't make a habit out of breaking promises.

So, let me start off with this little disclaimer. First off all, I'm not a writer by profession, and my college English professor may have even gone so far as to say I shouldn't even do it as a hobby. If you told me ten years ago that I would be writing a book someday I may have laughed in your face since I had enough trouble filling a ten page term paper. I have never considered myself a bad writer, and I always believed I had a firm grasp on the English language. Although, I'm sure there are more then a few of my past college professors who would argue to the contrary. The main objective of this book is to get my feelings across on paper so you can feel what I have felt. I'm pretty sure though this is something all authors try to do, so if I can reach that goal just a little then I will have met my first objective.

My second clarification is that I am not a trained or self-proclaimed emotional therapist. What I am is a person just like you who has gone through a life altering tragedy and come out on the other side. I may have come out better than most people, but worse than some others. The main thing is that I'm through it, and if something has happened to you, you can get though it too. Everyone must be allowed by those around them to feel the way they want to feel, and act the way they want to act as long as they are not a danger to themselves or anyone else. All people grieve differently and we must be given the freedom to express this in our own way. Now this does not mean we should let the people we love self-destruct before our eyes by becoming violent or abusing drugs.

However, what we do need to do is let them progress at their own pace. One of the things I like to say is, you really need to take that tragedy off the shelf and kick it around until you have worked yourself through the natural process of healing. There may be times when you want to leave it up on the shelf somewhere tucked way in the back to collect dust, but for God's sake don't. You have to face your fears. You must deal with, and overcome the past. You need to pick it up and toss it around until it isn't as heavy anymore. Because just like people, the longer they just sit around the heavier they get, but you know what? When you're picking it up and tossing it around, you are growing emotionally and spiritually stronger than you ever thought you could be. Without allowing yourself to work though your emotions they will keep coming out when ever hard times come up, and they will be much harder to handle then. When a person has not adequately dealt with events in the past they are almost always paralyzing to them in the future.

My emotions and thoughts on these events have changed quite a bit since the night my wife Michelle was murdered. Sure bad things are going to happen and there is very little we can do to stop them. No matter how much we protect ourselves and our families people are going to die, houses are going to burn, jobs are going to be lost, and the people around us are not going to behave the way we want them to.

However, it is not the WHAT happens to us, but HOW we handle it that determines what our character is. There are two directions you can go, one will destroy your life and your relationships, and the other will strengthen it. I stood at that intersection for a while trying to decide which way to turn. Let me tell you from that intersection both paths don't look the same. In the beginning each path is filled with obstacles but the wrong path seems like the easier one. On the wrong path you can put all that has happened behind you, and live off the anger and fear that has been generated by it. Sure, you don't have to face reality, but you face a lonely, fearful, and self-destructive existence. Sometimes the anger in my heart was so intense I wanted nothing more then to take the road to nowhere. I wanted to become a society dropout, but too many people were standing in front of me, and they would not let me go. My parents, my extended family and friends, my current wife, and the hope and love of God stopped me from going down that path and today I am thankful they did. The right path requires too much work, too much pain, and too much time. Yeah, maybe but, it is like Robert Frost said in his poem "The Road Not Taken" it is the path you take that will make all the difference. Once you deal with the events and emotions in your life you gain a wider prospective of why God placed you here in the first place, and you can allow God's blessings to work in you.

When our feelings sit around too long and get too heavy one day you will not be able to lift them anymore, then one of two things will happen. Whenever you hear of a situation that reminds you of what has happened you will not be able to cope, and you will no longer be in your control of your own emotions. Believe me in the age of modern media these things will come up. Events that took place shortly after Michelle died, like the O.J. Simpson trial, the Oklahoma City bombing and the Columbine High school shootings set me off pretty good. More recently of course the terrorist attacks on the World Trade Center and the Pentagon have unfortunately added thousands of people to the list of individuals who have tragically and needlessly lost someone they loved through the evil and heartless acts of another. This doesn't include the countless other local and national news stories that have provoked my emotions.

If you have gone through something like this there can be a feeling of hopelessness or anxiety that follows after such events. However, once you have achieved a sense of emotional healing you will feel mostly great compassion, understanding and love for those who have suffered.

I think what is the most damaging to your long-term emotional health is; you may never let joy or hope in your life again. Therefore your life becomes empty, and you fall in with so many in our society who blame the events in their lives for their, emotions, actions, or inaction.

I know this because my grandmother, who is a woman I loved dearly, was one of those people. When she was seven years old her mother past away, and until the day she died in her eighties, she still blamed everything bad in her life on this event. Worst yet my grandmother also claimed she was unable to experience happiness of any kind in her life, and felt no one else should either. All because of the death of her mother, she had been unwilling to deal with this her whole life. To her, life is something that is to be endured, just a series of bad events linked together by loneliness and despair. I know God never intended life to be this way.

Well if you don't feel you have the strength to handle it on your own you can always hide behind a bottle of pills or alcohol. Why not? So many other people do it in America today. Mind altering drugs are our country's "quick fix" to our emotional problems without having to face them head on. I understand that many people use prescription drugs temporarily while they are trying to get at the root of their problem and then stop, and I feel this is okay for some people. However, I also know that far too many people become dependent on these drugs to get through life and are never willing to go head to head with their emotions because that would be too hard, and too painful.

I'm sorry if I am offending anyone who feels that altering your mind on a daily basis with drugs is the only way out, but too bad. You have to learn to live without them. I always thought I was able to experience true joy, but I never truly appreciated joy until I had really experienced real pain, anger, and sadness. We all must see the range of human emotions to understand what makes life so beautiful. I tell you the truth, you can never get from a bottle what a kind word or a smile from a stranger can give you in your moment of sadness.

During my recovery, I went through the whole spectrum of emotions. There were days I didn't want to get out of bed because I was so depressed, and this was the time that I thought the most about killing myself. There were times I was so angry I felt all I wanted to do was physically hurt someone. I felt I had so much anger and adrenaline in me I could kill a man three times my size with my bare hands. Other days I was so scared and alone all I wanted was to be a little kid again in the protecting arms of my mother, and these times I would cry for hours. This range of emotions went on for almost three years at progressively less intensity. Although I refused to take prescription or illegal drugs, I used alcohol much more than I would like to admit, to escape or take the edge off the rough times.

Today I don't have these thoughts or needs anymore. My point is, unless I was able to freely go through all my emotions and the natural stages of grief, I would never have been able to fully appreciate the beauty and richness of the life God has given me.

Before Michelle died I was a different person, not a bad person, but different. My priorities were different, and although I thought of myself as intelligent I wasn't as aware of the feeling of those around me. I thought I followed the will of God. I wanted to be a good husband and father, work at the same company for forty years, maybe get a house in Florida when I retire like all New Yorkers did, and die of natural causes, nothing too fancy. Although the dreams I had in high school and early childhood where much grander than this "simpler" existence I felt okay with this. As things would turn out, the "simple" existence was not to be, but instead I was about to face one of the most frightening, evil, and difficult periods of my life.

Out of this experience I gained tremendous emotional growth. I must say after all things are considered I like who I have become. I don't look at the world through rose-colored glasses, but I am still an optimist. I see beauty in the world, which previously went unnoticed. Most of all I respect and cherish life, not only of those whom I love, but all life.

When I see on the evening news that someone has died, they are no longer just a story, but someone loves that person. They are someone's mother, father, wife, husband, or child. They all mean something to someone who loves them. This has always been true, but in a time when most people in the world are strangers to you, death becomes just another statistic. However, I can tell you first hand each statistic stands for something far greater...a life.

CHAPTER 1

I will never forget the day we met, it was New Year's Eve 1991. This was the first New Year my best friends and I were all twenty-one and we were going to have a good time. Rick, Todd, and I have been friends since Junior High, and this was really going to be a big night for us. I remember that age being such a milestone in my life, but in reality, at that age we were at the halfway point between being men and boys. We had gotten tickets to go to this club in downtown Rochester called Heaven. The night would include champagne, a buffet, and we hoped a lot of young women. I know what you are thinking... uh huh, so they met at a night club I know where this is going, but not so fast, after all it was New Year's Eve, and it happened to be the last time Michelle and I would ever go to a night club.

Anyway, my friends and I were sitting at the bar, and up walks this cute little girl with big hair, and big beautiful brown eyes. We made eye contact and she smiled at me. Now I don't know if its physically possible, but I'm pretty sure at that moment my heart skipped a beat. Then she turned and walked away, so after taking a few moments to gather my thoughts I went right back to talking with Rick and Todd. Besides, it was early and we had not even seen half the women in the place yet, so there was no reason to be in a hurry.

After a couple of drinks the boys and I were feeling pretty confident, and now it was time to dance. To avoid the whole embarrassing thought of having to ask a woman who was sitting on the sidelines to dance we had come up with a brilliant idea. All we needed to do was find a group of three or more woman already dancing and we could just jump in. I must say it was an absolute stroke of genius.

We spotted a group of girls on the floor who looked like they would really enjoy dancing with the three of us, so as planned we jumped in. At first it seemed to be working rather well, but soon the ladies started rolling their eyes and whispering to each other. Could it be they didn't appreciate my John Travolta, Saturday Night Fever choreography? Well by the end of that song the ladies danced their way far away from us, and there we were three guys in the middle of the dance floor. Huh, I don't understand what could have gone wrong, it sounded like the perfect plan on paper.

However, persistence was the key, things did eventually work out for us. As it so happened there was a group of young women on the dance floor who had the same idea we had. I was dancing with this girl, and I looked to see if Todd and Rick were still close by. There was Todd dancing with the beautiful big haired brown eyed girl, and I was thinking "Hey, way to go bud, she is a keeper." (That was how I talked when I was young). When I looked over at the two of them the girl and I made eye contact again, and she just smiled and turned her head back toward Todd. There was just something about her I was drawn to.

When the song ended all of us agreed we would split up to get drinks for the New Year's toast before midnight, but we would meet again before the clock struck twelve. However, when the time came to meet again I couldn't find the girl I was dancing with, and then I ran into her again, the big haired beautiful brown-eyed girl was now standing right in front of me.

"Did you see the girl I was dancing with earlier?" I asked.

"I don't know where she is, why do you ask?" she replied.

"It's two minutes until the New Year, and I need someone to kiss."

She then looked at me with a smile, her head was to one side, and she raised her shoulders slightly and said, "Well, if you like... you can kiss me."

And kiss her I did. When the clock struck twelve...we kissed. I'm pretty sure it lasted two hours, but I know we lost some time in there somewhere. Wow, this was it I thought, and I was in love with Michelle Lentine from that moment on.

Up until then there was never a woman to ever come into my life who meant as much to me as Michelle Lentine. She had a way about her that would light up a room with her presence because she was always so full of life. Michelle would always make whomever she was talking to the most important person in her life at that moment; so for this reason people seemed to really feel at ease around her. She would always get so excited when she was talking with people she cared about. Michelle had this little giggle whenever she was happy or excited and I don't know anyone who could resist her smile. She was honest, trustworthy, and a friend everyone could depend on, but above all else, Michelle truly walked with God. She had a genuine understanding of what Jesus meant when He said to take care of the least among you. So, for all these reasons and much more I fell deeply in love with her.

All this may seem a bit hard to believe, but it is true. Michelle was a genuine "giving soul." She had a career as a sign language interpreter for students with multiple sensory losses. In other words she communicated with children who were both deaf and blind in a way that most people never could. Children were able to experience the world outside through her. Just watching Michelle with one of her students would make me so proud of her. Michelle had a deep personal connection and genuine love for these kids. There were times when she would come home from work and just shed tears for these children. No matter how much she did she always wanted to do more for them.

There was one child Michelle dealt with on a one to one basis more then any other. Her name was Christina. She was a deaf and blind eight year old with a book full of questions in her mind about the world around her. Michelle felt so close with her as she would hold her little hands and sign into them so Christina may know what Michelle was seeing. There were times Michelle and I would take Christina on a Saturday afternoon to the park.

Christine would ask, "Where are we?"

"At the park." Michelle would sign to her.

"What does it look like?"

Michelle would take here hands and tell her how beautiful the green grass was, and how there were children on the swings and playing baseball.

"Who is with us?" She would ask. Michelle would do the sign for sweetheart in her hand. Then Christina would smile and say, "Hi Joey."

There was one Saturday evening Michelle and I took Christina to Catholic Mass. From what I understand Christina hated to go to church mainly because she would have to sit in the dark for 45 minutes to an hour and be totally quiet. It must have been torture for the poor girl not being able to see or hear just sitting there in a room full of people but unable to communicate or understand what was going on. Michelle would not have that, when she told Christina we were going to church that little girl pitched a fit. However, from the moment we walked through the church doors Michelle "signed" every word of what was said by everyone who participated. Christina was beside herself with excitement. It was as if she had discovered a whole new world because finally she understood what went on inside those church doors.

In the summer of 1991 Christina would still go to school, but not the same school she went to all year. Because of the lack of students attending in the summertime the Rochester City School District would send all the kids to one or two schools for practical economic reasons. The school Christina was sent to was in a neighborhood affectionately referred to as Bull's Head. This was an economically deprived area with one of the highest crime rates in the city. Although the school grounds were well protected, the surrounding area could be quite dangerous at times.

One afternoon I went to meet Michelle for lunch and a few of her students joined us under a tree in the schoolyard. There was this one child I remember, a very clever seventh grader in a wheel chair that lived only a few miles from the school. He told me of the time when he was sitting in his wheelchair just outside his family's apartment when two teenagers picked him up, set him on the curb, and stole his chair.

This was a very rough part of town, and even though this worried Michelle and myself, Michelle insisted she had to go for Christina. If Michelle wanted she did not have to work at all in the summer, but she chose to. It did not matter that she felt unsafe or that the working conditions were tough because it was more important for her to be there for Christina and the other children. Michelle shed tears for a lot of her students. She became deeply involved emotionally in their lives. Michelle was the teacher her students would remember most because she brought her heart to her job everyday.

Michelle had many talents, besides her incredible gift of sign language. She was also an extremely good entertainer. That girl could sing and play the piano like no one I ever knew. When I say sing, I don't mean the way most of us do in the shower or in the car, I'm talking operatic. Michelle could sing the part of Christine from *Phantom of the Opera* just as good if not better than anyone who had ever played the part on Broadway or around the world. Those of you who are familiar with that show can understand what I'm saying, no exaggeration that girl could sing.

I went with Michelle and her mother once to a church wedding where the two of them sang at the ceremony. They sounded so beautiful together. I don't remember all the songs they sang together, but the one that remains in my heart today is "Ave Maria, " I can still hear Michelle sing that song so beautifully, and when I close my eyes I can see her up in the choir loft standing by her mother singing that sad song with such a feeling of contentment in her eyes. I know singing with her mother was one of the things that gave Michelle the greatest joy.

Michelle was no slouch on the piano either; she was a proficient and flawless classical music pianist. Her little fingers would be going a mile a minute up and down that keyboard perfectly playing a classic piece by Chopin or Mozart. Since her hands were smaller than average she had to move much quicker, but you could never tell. Her mother said Michelle had wowed audiences at piano recitals ever since she was four years old.

One of the best things was Michelle's ability to overlap her talents. For instance her extremely patient and thorough teaching style went very well with her love for music. Her mother Catina owned and operated a piano school, where Michelle and a few other teachers would give lessons at people's homes, and she really enjoyed putting two of her great loves together, teaching and music.

Rochester has a big amateur theater circuit; this is a fact I did not know until I met Michelle. She was very involved in theater doing one show after another after another. She loved it. She loved getting in front of the crowds to sing and dance. She was in the amateur productions of *The Sound of Music, The Music Man, The Wizard of Oz,* and *You're a Good Man Charlie Brown.* She would do them all, and she never failed to land a part in any show she tried out for. However, it was often disappointing for her when she did not get the lead role in any of these productions, but she was still just as enthusiastic to have a part in the chorus.

These were just a few of her many true gifts, but the thing that most stands out to those who knew her was, her true faith and love for God. Now there were many people who may not know what it was about her that shined from her very being, but they knew it was something, and it was something very special. You see Michelle followed the lessons taught to us by our Savior Jesus Christ, to treat others, as she wanted to be treated. She would never judge anyone, or say a harsh word. She gave freely of herself, and her only reward was the good it would make her feel for helping another. Above all, she had a very tender and special place in her heart for those with disabilities, particularly those with hearing loss.

It used to make her so mad when people she knew would just try to push the deaf aside, and use horrible terms like "deaf and dumb". Michelle was able to do something very few hearing people can or are willing to do, at least those who do not have someone in their family who is deaf, but she tapped into them. Michelle taught me that the deaf were highly intelligent, deep thinking people who had feelings and dreams just like the rest of us. She felt great pain for the children she worked with, not because they were deaf, but because all they wanted was to be heard and have their dreams and goals taken seriously. What she did for a living was not a job for her, but instead it was her life and she needed those children to feel complete.

Because of her genuine goodness people wanted to be around her. They wanted to share in her glow, that special something that made her so loving toward others. In spite of all these wonderful things, she was only human and had her weaknesses and hard times like everyone else.

When Michelle was around eleven or twelve years old her father Larry died after a long fight with cancer. She watched her once strong and protective father become very weak before her eyes. Soon after her father's death Michelle, her mother Catina, and older sister Dena moved in with Catina's parents.

This was a difficult period in her life I know. Here she was at one of the most difficult ages for any child going from a little kid into being a young adult. Michelle took it in stride though. She would focus her attention on other things by becoming more involved in her music and in church. A common hang out for her was the convent attached to her Catholic high school. Michelle became friends with many of the nuns, who she says treated her with great love and understanding. She told me many times she had always wanted to be a nun, but it was a good thing for me she hadn't.

I know from what Michelle would tell me growing up after her dad died was hard, but after that tragedy she chose to take the road of wanting to give to others. This is a road not every child takes after the death of a parent or a divorce. I admired her for that, and she helped me to realize no matter if my father and I fought a lot or not, at least he loved me and was there for me when I needed him to be. She was right. I sometimes did not know how fortunate I was. When we met I was twenty-two years old, and never suffered the loss of a family member through death.

CHAPTER 2

Michelle and I started dating after that fateful New Year's Eve and we fell quite hard for one another. I was living in Buffalo, New York where I was working at FedEx as a driver and attending collage at SUNY Buffalo. Michelle lived back in Rochester with her mother and grandparents. From my apartment to her house was about seventy-five miles. The first few weeks I would travel up to see her only on the weekends. It worked out well because my parents lived on the west side of Rochester and I would drive in Friday after work and stay until Monday morning when I would drive back to go to class.

However, it did not take long before I started making trips on Thursday nights, then Wednesdays, and Tuesdays. By mid March I was for all intents and purposes living in Rochester and commuting back to Buffalo everyday for work and school. Needless to say my grades started to suffer, and after awhile school became my lowest priority. The most important part of my life was Michelle, and nothing else mattered, but I never missed a day of work.

About this time a few well intentioned FedEx co-workers and managers started filling my head with ideas about a career with the company. From what I was led to understand a college degree was not an important piece of paper when it came to working at the company, but what really mattered were the years you actually attended college. So, if you had four years of college this was almost as good as having a degree. I was now in my final semester of my fourth year, but unfortunately I was another year from graduation. My junior year of college I transferred from Kent State University in Ohio to SUNY Buffalo to be closer to home and lower some of my parent's college expenses. In the transfer I lost some credits, and not to mention I dropped a few classes here and there which put me two semesters behind. I was young, in love, and making really good money for someone my age, but I was about to make a big mistake.

Well I'm sure you know where I'm going with this one. That's right, the following May I applied for a transfer with FedEx to Rochester. I told my parents and most everyone I would attend school again back home to finish my degree, but in my heart I knew I would not be going back full time again. I took a couple classes at Nazareth Academy a catholic college in Rochester the following fall, but I just wasn't into school any more, so a couple of C's later and I was done. I was now ready to focus my attention on a management career with FedEx, and to being Michelle's husband. My mother wasn't too pleased, but my father was proud I chose a career with FedEx. He only wished, that I'd discovered my true purpose in life before he and mom spent thirty thousand dollars on my education.

Anyway, in mid-June 1991 just six months after Michelle and I first danced on New Years Eve I moved back to Rochester to live with my parents so I could be closer to Michelle. The job I took as a freight handler with FedEx was a step down on the corporate ladder from my previous job as a driver, but I was now in a full time position and happy to have it. I also had a wonderful opportunity to work under my father who was one of the men in charge of loading and unloading the airplanes. We grew really close during this time and I will always be thankful for that time in my life.

I was barely home a month before I started shopping for an engagement ring. I was anxious. I figured... why wait, the sooner we get married the better. By this time Michelle and I were inseparable. I worked nights not starting until seven p.m. most days, and she would get out of her job at the school by three p.m. I would go to see her everyday before work, and needless to say it was difficult getting to work on time. Both of us talked of marriage and I knew by July if I asked her to marry me she would most definitely say, "YES". So one Saturday with a ring in my pocket I set out to propose.

I really wanted to take her out to dinner that night. I envisioned a romantic candle light table in a quiet corner of our favorite Italian restaurant. I would look over at her and she at me, and it would be an evening we both would cherish forever. However, this was not to be. I went to her house with the ring in my pocket, but Michelle did not want to go out to dinner that night. Instead she wanted us to stay at home. She was tired and going out was the last thing she wanted to do. Her family had gone to church and she decided it would be nice to order take out and rent a movie or two and just enjoy each other's company by relaxing.

No matter what I said I could not get her to go out. The ring was just burning a whole in my pocket. I couldn't keep it another night. I was a nervous wreck. She wanted to watch TV for a while before we ordered out, and I figured I might be able to still persuade her. I was really trying to be careful not to be too insistent because then she might suspect something. Since I had been there she had already asked me a few times if I was okay. We sat on the couch I don't remember what we were even watching on TV, all I could think about was the ring, and how I was going to get her out of the house to give it to her.

"What is wrong...are you okay?" Michelle asked me with her nose wrinkled up.

"Sure" I said nervously like I was trying to hide something, "I'm fine, why do you ask?"

"You're just acting weirder than usual like something's up," she said.

"Up? No nothing's up...I just would like to go out to eat that's all, wouldn't you?"

"No, come on, let's just cuddle here for a while. We can order something to eat in a bit."

Great! She wanted to cuddle I thought what is the deal with cuddling. This was no time to cuddle, I had serious business, and cuddling would throw me off track. Besides, I was concerned she might notice the ring box in my pocket if she got too close. That's right, I left it in the box. So we are sitting there, and I asked one more time....

"So, are you sure you don't want to go out?" I asked, this was my last ditch effort.

"Yes, why do you and to go out so badly?" She asked.

I reached in my pocket pulled out the ring and said the first thing that came to my mind.... "Here."

My stunning silver tongue at such a romantic moment left her speechless, or maybe it was the ring. She was ecstatic, her jaw dropped open and she started to tear up, and then she through her arms around me.

"Well" I said " so what do you think, will you marry me?"

"Yes, yes I'll marry you."

I guess it isn't so much how you get there as long as you do.

So, there we were just seven months after we met, we were now engaged. I guess I could not help myself I was in love. Here I was just twenty-two years old, and I thought I had life all figured out. I had someone to love, and a career on the upswing. This was it.

By October of that same year we moved in together. We shared a small one-room apartment about three miles from my parent's house. Things were going very well for us. We enjoyed our first Christmas together in that apartment.

CHAPTER 3

The year 1992 was great for the both of us. Our relationship was growing stronger everyday, and we were learning more about each other. I received a promotion at work to courier and I began my management training. Michelle was doing really well at her careers as both an interpreter and piano teacher, and no doubt both of us believed life was beginning to work out pretty good for us.

Much of the year for us was spent planning for our wedding, which Michelle and I had set for December 5th of that year. Christmas was her favorite holiday, and she wanted our wedding to take place during the Catholic celebration of Advent. (Advent is the tradition, in which the church relives the preparation period for the coming of Christ, and it lasts a month or so before Christmas, being four Sundays. During this time the church alter is adored with purple and its clergy wear purple robes.) She had also wanted Christmas trees, wreaths, and a beautiful white blanket of snow on the ground. For Michelle there could be no other time that would be quite so perfect as this time of year.

Like most young husbands to be I thought all of Michelle's ideas were just wonderful, and I was content for her to make the decisions on everything. However, as you can expect my opinion was always asked for, yet it was often ignored, and I was brought in to do a lot of the leg work, you know phone calls, meetings with caterers, and so on. To add another element of difficulty to this painstaking process, my sister and I were also trying to plan a surprise party for our parent's twenty-fifth wedding anniversary to take place in October. Sometimes the situations became a little tense between, my sister Theresa, Michelle, and myself, but Theresa and I always had a good relationship so a few squabbles over buffet choices were not going to do any damage to us. In the end we put on a really great celebration for my parents, and Theresa and I were able to make my parents very happy which is all that really matters.

For our wedding however, I had one major hurdle to get over. Michelle wanted to get married in the Catholic Church, and since the time that I had met her I started attending Catholic mass once again. I was born into a Catholic family, and I received baptism as an infant and first communion as a second grader, but the sacraments stopped there. I was missing one important one along the way, confirmation. This sacrament takes place when you are a teenager, and is a right of passage for a young Catholic when he or she becomes a full-fledged adult and a responsible member of the church.

When I was about 12 years old my family stopped going to the Catholic Church and began attending a Baptist Church. We attended there for almost five years, and I had a lot of wonderful and blessed experiences there. My parents, my sister and I each became saved born again believers, and began to develop a one on one relationship with Jesus. However, after a few years, and a couple of pastors, church politics started to get in the way, and we felt like we no longer belonged there, so my family left the church altogether. God was still a part of our family life, but church was not.

I wanted to reconcile this. I wanted to once again be a part of the church community, and Michelle's strong ties with the church made it extra important to me. Before I was going to be able to be confirmed though I would have to attend class for a few months to better understand what it is to be an adult member of the church. Since most people taking this class were pre-teenagers I was not looking forward to going through this process, but there were night classes given for adults who missed confirmation the first time around. I worked nights, which made it impossible for me to attend class on a regular basis for months at a time. All was not lost however. Father Bush, the priest at Holy Spirit church made special arraignments to tutor me one on one until I learned what I needed to know to go through confirmation.

As you can imagine I was a bit intimidated about this idea. Sure I sat in Father Bush's office a few times with Michelle by my side, she just happened to always know all the rights things to say. But me, by myself, sitting directly across from a priest being asked questions, and not depending on other students to answer any of them with not even the anonymity of a confessional booth to protect me was extremely nerve racking.

Well all my nightmares about it turned out to be nothing. Although, it did get a little tense whenever the subject of unmarried couples co-habiting came up. Especially since Father Bush had known and loved Michelle for so long, at times I felt like I was in the room with her father. Any discomfort I felt in the end was worth it. I was confirmed in May of that year and now I was caught up "sacrament wise" with the Catholic Church, and able to get married as a full-fledged member of the church.

To me the plans for the wedding started to become too detailed. Previously I had had no idea all that went into the planning for just a one-day celebration. There was the reception location, sit down or buffet, colors of gowns, napkins, musicians, who to invite and so on. Michelle wanted me to have involvement it every last one of these details. Many of which I could have cared less about. My main concerns were, the honeymoon, food, drink, family, and friends, and not necessarily in that order.

For Michelle of course one of the most important things was the music. We had some of the very best professional and amateur musicians play at our wedding. At the Church we had a string quartet, and at the reception we had a band and a classical pianist play during dinner. It was a good thing she knew all these people who generously offered to either discount their services or give them away entirely as a wedding gift to us. Otherwise, we would not have been able to afford anything else.

The reception was at the downtown Holiday Inn, and the room was all glass overlooking the Genesee River. I must admit it was a very classy event. Michelle had dreamed of this day her entire life, and I wanted to be sure she received the wedding day her heart always wanted. I must admit I had very serious reservations about the expense of such an elegant wedding. We had to cut our guest list way down so we could keep within our family's budget. My parents paid for a lot of the wedding, and I often found myself in a very difficult spot between my mother's ideas and Michelle's. In the end there was a lot of compromising and everything turned out beautifully, and in retrospect I'm thankful for all the wonderful memories that day produced.

The night before our wedding the air was cold as December in Rochester usually was, but there was not one flake of snow on the ground. As a matter of fact there had not been any snow yet that year. After the wedding rehearsal and dinner Michelle went to stay with her mother at her grandparents' house, while I was going to stay at my parents' house. Todd and Rick who each played important roles in my wedding took me out that night to have a little fun. Our last stop was Nick Tahoe's "Home of the Garbage Plate" which was a place we had frequented most every weekend for much of our teenage years. I won't go into the explanation of a garbage plate because even the detailed literary style of Hemingway could not do it justice.

Anyway, while we were there I used the payphone to call Michelle. "How are you doing peaches," I asked, " you're still going to show up tomorrow, right?"

"Of course I am...I really miss you, I don't think I will be able to sleep tonight without you here with me" she said.

"Don't worry sweetie it is just one night. After tomorrow we will be married and you will never sleep without me ever again."

"I know. I can't wait. Please be careful leaving there tonight, they say it's going to snow."

"Really, well that's cool, so, I guess you may get your wish after all of having the first winter's snow on our wedding day."

"That's what I'm hoping for. I love you and I'll see you tomorrow. I'm really excited and probably won't sleep a wink."

"Me too sweetie, I love you and you know after tomorrow you will be Mrs. Forte."

"I know, I just love the sound of that," she said with a longing sigh in her voice.

Rick and Todd were yelling for me too hurry up, "you will have the rest of your life to be with her so lets go," they yelled. As we were heading home the snow began to fall.

By the next morning the sun was shining high in the sky it had stopped snowing, and we had gotten nearly six inches of fresh snow overnight. I was even a little worried some of our guests may have trouble making it, but this was Rochester where it snows six months a year so no one had any trouble getting there. It was truly a blessing I thought a sign that God would be with us in our marriage always, and he personally was giving us his blessing and approval. I remember really believing that with all my heart. Michelle and I both thought we were soul mates and that God had brought us together. Even if we did not meet on New Year's Eve almost two years earlier, God would have found a way to bring us together anyway.

I arrived at church about an hour or so before the wedding. As the guests were all coming in I took the time to walk up to everyone I could to say hello. I really loved this. It was the happiest day of my life. Rick and I knelt down in the front pew to pretend we were praying instead we were just talking.

Rick put his hand in front of his mouth and mumbled to me, "This is it buddy, are you sure you want to go through with it?"

"Oh yeah, I'm going through with it." I replied.

"Alright then, I'll be right there for you."

We stood off to the side as the music started to play and the procession started down the aisle. About then I started to get the butterflies in my stomach. I couldn't believe it. I was getting married, and just as I was approaching my spot at the front of the alter I saw Michelle coming in escorted by her mother. She looked beautiful, and at that moment I could not believe how blessed I was. She was trembling and tears were rolling down her face. Even after all the shows I had seen her perform in I had never before seen her so nervous, but after her mother gave Michelle's hand to me her shaking started to calm down. Later she would tell me she was so nervous that she just wanted to run down the aisle to me. Usually stage fright was not something Michelle suffered from.

Our wedding ceremony and reception were wonderful, and everything went off without a hitch. Michelle even sang a couple of songs at our reception, and I remember Rick turning to me to say that our kids would have the most beautiful lullabies sung to them one day. He was right. She had a beautiful voice, and I remember thinking that night what a wonderful mother she was going make.

CHAPTER 4

The next morning we got up early to catch a flight to Orlando, Florida. We were going to spend a week in Disney World. Michelle and I stayed right on Disney property at a resort called Dixie Landings, which was modeled after the great Southern Plantations. We had a blast there. I think we did almost everything you could do there. The park was decked all out for Christmas, and we visited every little Christmas gift shop we came across. Michelle and I felt like two kids who just happened to be married to each other.

On the flight back to Rochester Michelle had a few tears in her eyes. She did not want to leave, because after all the planning over the past year for our wedding and the trip, it was all coming to an end with this final ride home. Now that did not mean we were not both excited to spend the rest of our lives together, but it's kind of like the day after Christmas. You spend so much time planning for the wedding and imagining what it would be like, and when the day finally comes its even better than you imagined, but it passes so quickly.

When we arrived back home that beautiful first snow we had experienced a week earlier turned the city back into the frozen tundra we remembered from the year before. After being in Florida only a week we found it pretty easy to get used to the mild weather of the South, and we were not looking forward to the next five months or so of bitter cold.

My parents met us at the airport, and my mother was so excited to see us. She wanted to tell Michelle and I all the wonderful things people had said to her about our wedding. Mom was so funny, as my wife and her were talking about memories from the wedding as if it had taken place years before. It was sweet though. My mother and father thought of Michelle more as a second daughter than a daughter-in-law, and I loved the fact that the two women I loved most in the world loved each other too.

In early October before the wedding Michelle and I had moved from the apartment by my parents, and moved into a two bedroom duplex about fifteen miles away. We really loved it. They were older town homes, but it was in a great well-established suburban neighborhood. There was a lot of room too. There were two bedrooms upstairs, and the living room was big enough for Michelle's Baby Grand piano. There was even a full basement. We thought we were living pretty well, and God had really blessed us. I figured when I finished my Management program at FedEx I could put in for a transfer with the company down in Florida. Michelle was all for the idea as long as the city we moved to had active amateur theater groups.

Michelle's mother had stayed at our place while we were gone mostly to care for our cat Jake, but also to have a little bit of time to her self. When we walked in the door the conversation my mother and Michelle were having continued adding Michelle's mother too. And so it went...wasn't this beautiful? So and so said she really loved it...I started to cry when...that was hilarious...and on and on.

Once that conversation was over my mother-in-law told me a family had moved into the townhouse adjoining ours. Up until that point that half of the duplex had been unoccupied since we moved in. She told me they had moved in over the weekend and she saw the poor guy trying to move a washing machine by himself up the sidewalk.

Our new neighbors were a young African-American family with two young children. Michelle and I were relieved to have a family move in next-door and not a bunch of college kids. In our previous apartment the walls were paper thin, and the neighbors above us were up until all hours of the night making a racket. One of the main reasons we moved to this new place was because there would not be anyone living above us. We thought maybe next weekend after we had gotten settled in we would stop by to introduce ourselves to our new neighbors.

Thursday December 17th, four days after our return from our

honeymoon, I get a frantic call at work around nine p.m. It was Michelle, crying and very shaken up. "Joey, someone broke into our townhouse. Please, come home."

"My God, are you okay?" my heart was beating a hundred times a second at the very thought of anything happening to her or anyone being in our home.

"Yes, I'm fine. I wasn't even here when it happened. I just came home and the police were here. Someone had thrown a brick through the sliding glass door. Come home Joey, please I'm scared." She said as her voice was trembling.

"I'll be right there, I'm leaving now. Hang in there. I love you." I said.

"I love you too. Hurry, please."

When I arrived home about twenty minutes later there were two police cars there and Michelle's mother and grandparents came right over to be there for us.

I ran in the front door in a panic to see what had happened. It wasn't just a brick that was thrown through our back door, but one of those big cement blocks that weighed about twenty to twenty-five pounds. It did some real damage. That rear door was destroyed, and the brick had made a huge dent in the floor. Michelle said nothing had been taken, but whoever had come in turned over her underwear drawer and ransacked her panties. What was that all about? Why would someone break in to throw Michelle's panties around?

The police on the scene took pictures and notes. They told us these kinds of things happen and it was probably nothing to worry about because people who do these things never come back. They determined it was not a professional job because the person made so much noise, and was probably just doing in for the thrill. The police said they arrived at our townhouse no more than two or three minutes after the break in occurred, and only our neighbors were there because they were startled by the loud noise.

Our new neighbor from the adjoining townhouse came to our front door while the police were talking. He introduced himself to me as Leroy, and said he talked with Michelle before I got there. Michelle told me he was very nice and came right over as soon as he heard the crash, and he even saw the guys running away from the back of the townhouse and into the woods.

I was anxious, "You did see them Leroy? What did they look like? "

"I really couldn't tell, " Leroy said "but they looked like a couple of white teenage kids. I started to chase them, but they escaped into the woods."

"Well thanks. I really appreciate it." I said.

"Hey, no problem what are neighbors for. Don't worry about your wife here I'll look after things at night while you're working."

Knowing that he would be looking out for her after something like this had happened really made me feel better. We had this big guy who weighed about three hundred pounds living next door who was a family man, and I really felt glad he was next door looking out for us.

Over the next few weeks we got to know our neighbor a lot better because he kept coming over to our place, mostly in the evenings while I was at work. He would ask Michelle if he could borrow things like milk, butter and even money. Sometime after Christmas, Leroy asked Michelle if he could borrow twenty dollars to last him until he was paid the next week. Michelle was not too keen on this, but we figured we were helping out his family. If there were no young children involved that would have been different, but Michelle and I always had rationalized that we were doing something good for folks who needed a little help.

About three weeks had passed and Leroy had not paid us back the twenty dollars he borrowed and Michelle was getting a bit angry. He had told us when he was paid the next week we would get our money back. Well, she had enough. One Sunday afternoon she and I walked over to Leroy's to tell him it was time to pay us back. Michelle did all the talking, but I was standing right beside her on his front porch.

"Leroy," she said, " we need you to pay us back our money you borrowed now. You said it would only be a week until you could pay us back, but now it has been more than three."

He looked at us calmly and replied, "Alright." Then he went back inside for a minute or so and came out with a twenty-dollar bill. "Here." he shoves the bill in her face, and Michelle grabbed it.

We said thank you and left. Leroy did not come around our place for a few weeks after that. Either he was mad or he thought he had used up all our generosity towards him. No matter how he felt, it was peaceful for a while.

The peace however was short lived. It was now late January, and once again I received a disturbing call at work around nine thirty or ten p.m. It was Michelle and she was very distraught. The police had just left our apartment again.

Michelle started to explain to me the details of what had gone on only a few minutes earlier. She was upstairs in our bedroom getting ready for bed when the doorbell rang. Now this wasn't the pleasant ring someone may do when they stop by for a visit, but it was the alarming, jump out of your skin, type ring when someone hits the doorbell five or six times in just a few quick seconds. Then the person started pounding hard and frantically on the door and trying the doorknob to get inside. Michelle was getting very scared. The pounding and the ringing did not stop.

She tried to look out the window of our bedroom to see who it was. The front door was right under the window, but she could not see who it was because the person was standing too close to the house. The pounding started to move along the outside walls of the house until the person reached the back.

Poor Michelle was a nervous wreck. She started to panic and shake with fear. She did not know who it was outside and why they were trying so hard to get it. She picked up the phone to call 911. It was so loud that the operator on the other end could hear the pounding and doorbell ringing. Michelle crouched herself in the corner like a scared little girl. The 911 operator tried to calm her down and would not hang up until police arrived.

Then the ringing and pounding stopped, and the operator told Michelle the police had radioed her to say that they had arrived. Michelle stood up to look out the window to see two police cars parked in front of our apartment. She went down-stairs just as the officers were coming to the door. Standing between them with one officer holding his left arm and the other holding his right, was Leroy. "Do you know this man, miss? We caught him running away from your place here." one officer said.

"Michelle, tell them! We're friends!" Leroy pleaded. "Karen is in the hospital. She fell at work and I need your car to go see her at the hospital."

Michelle's fear had now turned to anger. "Leroy, what is the matter with you? Why couldn't you just knock? You scared me to death."

"I'm sorry I didn't mean to scare you, but I need to get your car to go to the hospital."

"Can't you just wait a little bit, Joe will be home and I'm sure he will be willing to take you." Michelle was not too keen on letting Leroy just take our car. We had a used Volvo that Michelle bought on her own a couple of years earlier, and she was not one to let others drive it. On the other hand though, she did feel very sorry for him, and two policeman were right there with him making her feel safe, so she gave him her set of keys.

When I got home Michelle was up waiting for me. She was very upset, and felt she was forced to give Leroy the car because of his pleading in front of the police officers, even though she did not want to I was trying to calm her down and make her relax. She wanted us to move right away. This was not the first time she mentioned it, but now she was feeling very scared living there and this time she really meant it. I was very angry myself at the way Leroy went about the whole thing. I understand he was upset, but unless he was a five year old in absolute terror I can't imagine that he could not gather enough composure to knock on the door like a normal person. Besides, if he was that distraught it was probably not a very good idea to be driving in the first place.

I waited up until after midnight when Leroy finally brought back the car. It was time I had a few words with our neighbor. Leroy had just about spent all my good will, and I was about to set some very serious ground rules. What he had put Michelle through that night was very disturbing, and I was not about to let it happen again.

He walked up to my front door with a half smirk on his face and his hand extended with Michelle's keys. I opened the front door and let him come into the living room.

"Hey, thanks for letting me borrow the car." he said "I got to the hospital just in time to sign the papers. Karen slipped and fell at work and lost the baby, and she almost died too. I had to sign the papers to have the doctors take the baby so Karen wouldn't die."

"Man, Leroy, I'm so sorry to hear that. I did not know Karen was even pregnant." My anger with him quickly turned into genuine concern.

"Well, there was nothing they could do. She wasn't pregnant very long. I'm just glad she's all right. The doctors say she'll be fine. Do you think you could give me a ride back to the hospital? I need to get back."

"Yeah, sure of course, I'll give you a ride." I ran up the stairs to tell Michelle where I was going. "Listen honey, I'm going to give Leroy a ride back to the hospital. Karen almost died tonight and she lost the baby she was carrying."

"Oh my God. Is she okay?" Michelle was very upset to hear this and even felt guilty for being so hard on him earlier.

"Yeah, she'll be fine. I'll be back soon. I love you."

"I love you too, please be careful."

Leroy and I got in the car, and headed out to the hospital. He said she was at Strong Memorial hospital about twenty miles away from where we lived. There were two other hospitals that were about half that distance from us, but I didn't think anything of it. Strong was one of the best hospitals in the county, so it was not odd that she would be there. Besides the ride would give Leroy and I time to talk.

I must admit that whatever he and Karen had just gone through took quite a bit of the sting out of what I was going to say. However, I still felt like I had to say something. "Leroy, no offense or nothing, but I would prefer you did not come around our place anymore to ask Michelle for anything when I'm not at home. You are making her very uncomfortable, and I don't like that. You know I work nights and I'm not there and this makes her uncomfortable enough, so I would like you to wait until I come home to ask for anything from now on."

"I understand. Karen feels unsafe too. She made me get an alarm that sounds like a barking dog to scare away anyone trying to get in. A few nights ago I set it off myself when I went downstairs in the middle of the night. That thing just started barking and I couldn't get it to shut off..."

Leroy seemed to understand where I was coming from. Even though he never came out and said directly that he would stop bothering Michelle, I had a feeling I got through to him. The rest of the ride we talked about football, the Bills mostly. He said he had season tickets and even asked me to go to a game with him next year. Leroy never bothered Michelle again.

CHAPTER 5

Sometimes I still wonder why bad things happen to us. Thankfully, for most of us these bad things tend to be minor, but there are events that can change your whole life forever. We all know people who, we may think, are not as kind or moral as we are, but somehow nothing bad ever seems to happen to them. These feelings of injustice are at their strongest when we feel something has happened to us that we do not deserve. Such is the case for me on the night of February 23, 1993, on the Catholic Holiday, Ash Wednesday.

It started off like any other day for me. I awoke around ten a.m., which was my normal time because I worked nights and often did not get home until after eleven p.m. I don't remember much of the morning until around one p.m. when my wife Michelle came home unexpectedly from work.

Her student was not at school that day so she was able to leave work early. Michelle had taken advantage of her time off by stopping to get her nails manicured before she came home. I was really very happy to see her because our different work schedules often kept us apart during the week. Still we didn't have much time together because I needed to be at work by two p.m., so Michelle spent that short amount of time with me while I was getting ready for work.

As I was getting ready to walk out the door she had made the suggestion that I should call into work so we could spend some time together. I never called in sick to work when I wasn't really sick because of the guilt I would feel. So, we kissed good-bye and told each other "I love you", and I headed out the door.

I remember sitting in the car just before I pulled away I looked up towards the front door of our apartment to see her with the familiar pout she always had when she felt sad. Michelle was looking at me with her big brown eyes, and her bottom lip pulled out over the top. She looked like a little girl standing there watching me leave. I only wish I knew then this would be the last time I would see her. I would have called in sick.

On my way to work I was trying to think of what to give up for Lent. For anyone not familiar with the Catholic Religion, Lent is the forty-day period between Ash Wednesday and Easter Sunday when it is customary to give up something you really love to show your devotion to Jesus Christ. I gave up the same old things I gave up every year chocolate and Coca Cola. At that time I was praying and making a commitment to God over this, and I remember feeling pretty good about my life that afternoon. I felt blessed, and most of all I felt I deserved it because I was a pretty good person.

Federal Express was the same as always that day. My pick up route was one of the least desirable routes at our station. It covered a forty-two square mile area north of the city. The size of the area and the number of stops I had generally kept me very busy, but I enjoyed the pace because my day went by much quicker. My grandparents also lived close by and I would try to stop there for my dinner break once a week or so. I would even have the opportunity to stop by my apartment before returning to the station on occasion, but we lived about ten miles out of the way. The days when I finished my route early and Michelle was home I would take the travel time off my dinner break and get to spend a half hour at home. On a good week I was able to do this once or twice. Even though no one else at work liked my route, to me it could not get much better.

This day however, I would not get the chance to go home for dinner. My day was fairly busy, as most Wednesdays were, and Michelle had play practice that evening. Around six p.m. I was able to call home at one of my regular stops. Packages were left at the receptionist's desk so I would usually take this opportunity to make a quick call home. Today I was hoping to catch Michelle before she had to leave for play rehearsal. Strangely enough I received a busy signal when I called home. We had call waiting on the phone, so I knew this generally did not happen, unless, Michelle had two people on the phone at once, or the phone was off the hook. So, I assumed it was either one of these two explanations, and I did not give it another thought.

I went on to complete my pickups that evening, and stopped for a pizza before I headed back to the FedEx station. I took the pizza into the truck where I eat as I read the evening paper. I ate half the pizza and saved half for Michelle. When I was finished I headed back to the station.

Once I got in the evening package sort was in full swing. I off loaded my truck, and went out to the airplane where my duty was to help load. Everything had gone off as planned as it had so many times before. The plane left on time and it was about time for me to go home.

Just like every night I called home just before I was ready to leave and again I received a busy signal. I really felt this was strange because it was about ten forty-five p.m. I asked someone in the office if there was word of any phone lines being down around town, and he did not seem to think so. In my head I concluded that our cat Jake must have knocked the phone off the hook. Our bedroom phone sat on the floor next to our bed at night, and during the day we would place it on the bed so we could reach it easier. Our bed was a waterbed so conceivably Jake could have knocked the phone when he jumped on our bed. This seemed like a pretty good explanation to me so I still wasn't very concerned.

I talked a little with my manager Scott and our station manager Vinny before leaving. I was going through FedEx's management training program, so we where discussing what I had left to do before I could complete the program. Scott and I had become really close over the past two years I was there. He had taught me a lot about managing at the company, and my father taught me everything I needed to know about the company's operations. I was told it would not be long before I could take the test that would make me eligible for promotion to management. Michelle and I looked forward to this time. I was hoping to get a transfer to somewhere in Florida soon. Both of us were pretty tired of the winters in Rochester and we did not want to endure many more.

I left the office around eleven p.m. and started home. When I pulled into our apartment parking lot the first thing I noticed was

Michelle's car was missing. I thought by eleven fifteen p.m. surely she would be home. However, the play she was in was opening in a week so it was not uncommon for them to stay late. I figured she would be home any minute.

I parked the car and headed up the snow-covered walk toward our front door. Like most days in February we had received about a half-inch of fresh snow that day. At the front door I noticed large boot prints in the snow on our front stoop. I thought maybe our building maintenance man had been to our apartment earlier that day or maybe the mailman. Usually only Michelle's footprints and my own can be found at the front door, but I wasn't too concerned. I proceeded to unlock the front door. When I was putting my key in the lock I noticed the front door was unlocked, and not closed all the way. Still I did not expect the worst, but I was puzzled. I thought to myself, how busy could Michelle have been to not even close the door all the way?

I stepped in the apartment and took off my boots. Jake, our cat, was sitting on the piano when I came in. He seemed to look fine. I put my lunch cooler and leftover pizza on the floor beside the front door. The stairs which lead to the second floor where located directly behind the front foyer. While I was standing there I could see that the light in our room was on, and I could also hear the television. As I walked up the stairs I could see the light from the television was flicking on the hallway wall. When I came to the top of the stairs I found the phone receiver in the hallway, so I picked it up. The spiral phone cord seemed to have been cut, by this time I did not know what was going on.

Right then I looked into our bedroom, and there she was. At that moment I felt my heart drop to my feet, and it was as if someone had hit me in the stomach. Everything seemed to be moving in slow motion. Michelle's body was lying face down on the floor by the foot of our bed with blood all around her. I ran to her and dropped to my knees. The whole time I was screaming her name at the top of my lungs, "My God Michelle.... what has happened...NO."

I knelt beside her and brought my face within inches of hers. Michelle's face was covered in blood, and I could hardly make out the features of her face. I looked at her body and she was naked. I noticed one wound in the center of her back. I touched her arm and tried to nudge her, but her whole body was stiff. I was probably only beside her for a few seconds, but every detail of how I found her is permanently burned into the back of my mind.

I stood up screaming and ran downstairs, I don't remember touching too many stairs on the way down. I headed toward the kitchen to use the phone, but the receiver was gone. I jumped into my work boots and ran out the front door. Every second of this time I was screaming, "God no....they killed her...they killed my Michelle". I was trembling as I ran to our neighbor Patty's house through the front yard. I fell in the snow a couple of times along the way. When I got to Patty's door I began pounding, and yelling "Help! Please help! They have killed Michelle." Patty answered the door and in a panicked tone of voice asked me what happened. I frantically screamed at her that Michelle was dead someone had killed her. Her mouth dropped open as she cupped her hands in front of her face.

I cannot remember if it was Patty or me who called 911, but I remember yelling hysterically on the phone that someone had killed my wife. I told the operator I was going back into the townhouse. She pleaded with me to stay where I was and wait for the police get there. Part of me really did want to go back into the house while another part of me was scared to death of what else I might find. I was almost thankful for the operator insisting that I stay out of the house.

When the police arrived I ran outside to meet them. They asked me what was wrong and where Michelle was. Everything felt like a bad dream ever since I laid eyes on Michelle's body. I couldn't believe this, and I wouldn't believe it. This was when I started thinking she may still be alive, so now that the police were there I wanted back in that apartment.

An EMU driver grabbed me by the arms and led me to the back of the ambulance. I sat down in the ambulance while a policeman guarded me to make sure I would not try to run back into the townhouse. I remember shaking and rocking back and forth for what seemed like hours.

Finally, the policeman emerged from the townhouse and walked straight over to me. I asked is she still alive! "No, I'm sorry", he said, "She is dead". My heart sunk again, there was no hope now. Michelle was gone and never coming back. Right then my life was changed forever, but little did I know that my life had already changed at about five forty-five p.m. that evening.

CHAPTER 6

The officers had taken me back to Patty's apartment so they could work undisturbed. Soon after that, my parents arrived. Both of them were crying and ran over to embrace me. My parents were very distraught. They were each very fond of Michelle, but at this moment I believe they were mostly concerned about me. They did not know what to expect when they got there, so they were very relieved to see me. We sat down on the couch as my parents tried to console me.

The next person I remember seeing was my neighbor Leroy. He walked in the front door with a puzzled look on his face to see what happened. When Leroy came in he walked straight over to hug me. While we where embracing he asked me what had happened, and I started to cry again. "They killed her Leroy, someone killed my Michelle," I said. To which he replied. "I know how you feel, my father was killed too".

I don't remember seeing him anymore that evening, but according to my family and other neighbors, he spent most of the evening talking with them. He talked about how close he was to Michelle and I, and how tragic it was that such a horrible thing like this could happen to her.

Soon after I talked with Leroy, the policeman who first responded to the call came in to bring me back outside. I had told him about the footprints I saw on the porch, and he wanted me to point them out to him. While we were outside I was introduced to Sgt. Mulkin. He was the detective who would be heading up Michelle's murder investigation.

Sgt. Mulkin was soft-spoken, and I could tell by the look in his eyes he was a compassionate man. He told he how sorry he was that we had to meet under these circumstances, and he seemed genuinely concerned about how I was doing. He asked if I would be able to accompany him to police headquarters to answer some background questions. Without much hesitation I agreed. Frankly, at this point I wanted to get out of there.

As we traveled to the Town of Greece police station I felt numb. The Sergeant and I may have been involved in small talk, but I really can't remember. All I do remember was staring out the window at the peaceful snow covered streets, and wondering what was I going to do now.

We arrived at the police station sometime after midnight. Sgt. Mulkin and I were alone to the best of my knowledge, so he took me into his office to talk. The questions he was asking where mostly about Michelle and myself. We talked in depth about what each of us did for a living, our relationship, and how the last few days we had together had been. I was starting to feel at ease for the first time that evening. I felt like I was helping him find out who killed her, and I was telling him everything he wanted to know.

When he asked me if I knew of anyone that may want to hurt her, I really could not think of any strong suspects. However, I did give him a few names of people she may have had contact with that day including students at the school where she worked and fellow cast members from the play she was performing in. Frankly, I could not imagine anyone who knew her who would want to kill her, but maybe the people I named could help the police somehow in the investigation.

Sgt. Mulkin was giving me every indication I was a big help to him, and strangely enough my mind was not focused as much on Michelle's murder, but on catching her killer. I did not have the ability at that time to piece any information together on my own because my mind was just too foggy at that point. I just kept answering his questions and seeking his none verbal approval, either he would nod his head or raise his eyebrows letting me know that I said something that may be of some help.

By this time it felt like we had talked for hours. Sgt. Mulkin then left the room to get me something to drink. While he was gone another investigator, Detective Lumpkin, came in to talk with me. He asked me more questions about the play Michelle was involved in. He wanted to know whom she hung around with, and if anyone of them had ever been to our apartment.

I knew most of her friends at the theater by face and a good many of them by first name. For this particular show she was car-pooling with a man whom I hadn't met before. I had every trust and confidence in Michelle and her judgment so I was not too concerned, but the more Detective Lumpkin and I talked about it, the stranger it started to sound. Maybe this guy could have been involved. Now we were getting somewhere. I supplied a solid lead and what seemed like some very good information. Pretty soon I felt they would have the guy who did this. However, things were about to get real ugly, and I was soon going to find myself on the defensive.

I was now left alone in the office. It had been quite some time since I arrived home to find my wife murdered. The sun was starting to come up, and I was hoping this whole night had been just a bad dream. Then the door opened and in walked Detective Lumpkin with a new guy, Sergeant Sullivan, and they where not happy. One of then said in a loud stern voice, "All right, time to cut the crap, we know you killed Michelle!"

I froze; I was in shock at what I was hearing. "What are you talking about?" I said with panic in my voice.

At this point I cannot remember who was saying what exactly, but this conversation was taking a horrible turn. They said, "Look Joe, its time to level with us. We know it was you. Come on, you said yourself Michelle was hanging around some guy in the theater you did not like because they where having an affair."

"What! I did not say anything about an affair. Michelle would never cheat on me." I yelled back.

"Come on Joe, we already know you used to slap her around, we have witnesses. Michelle even told her friends she was scared of you. Her friends will attest to that." Now I was starting to get angry with them. Everything I had told them was getting turned around and being thrown back at me, trying to make me out to be a liar. My mind started racing. Who were these witnesses? What friends had they talked to? Michelle wasn't scared of me was she?

"Who told you I hit her? I never laid a hand on her. What is going on here?" I said.

This bantering went on back and forth for a while. I did not know what to say anymore. I just kept defending everything they were accusing me of. When they would turn around something I said, and I would try to straighten it out again, but I felt I wasn't getting through to them. This heavy interrogation went on for what seemed like hours, but they finally left me alone again in the room for a while.

By now I was a nervous wreck. My heart was beating so fast I thought it would tear through my chest. I started running my hands over the top of my head pulling at the hair on my scalp. I kept pacing the floor talking to myself. "What was I going to do?" was all I could ask myself. I almost started to believe what they where telling me.

Just then, as if the first assault wasn't enough, all three of them walked in together. This time they where talking in a lower tone of voice. They would take turns talking with me, but now they had a theory.

"Okay Joe, here is what we think happened. You and your wife had a fight, and you were very jealous of this other guy she was seeing. One thing leads to another, and the next thing you knew...you had killed her. Joe, it's a crime of passion. It happens all the time. The DA may go easy on you."

"A crime of passion? My wife was brutally murdered! This was no crime of passion. I did not do this!" If it was at all possible I was now starting to feel even worse. "Didn't you check on the guy I told you about?"

"We checked into him, but he was clean. You are the only one who could possibly have done it, so why don't you just admit it. You will have a much better chance with the judge and the DA if you just admit what you did." They talked so confidently like they knew the whole story.

"What do you want from me?" I said almost begging for mercy.

"The truth," Detective Lumpkin said now in a very angry tone.

By this time each of them was starting to take on a different character in this interrogation. There was the angry cop, the even-tempered cop who only believes what he can see, and the one who was only looking out for my best interests.

"How are you going to look Michelle's mother in the face knowing you killed her daughter?" Detective Lumpkin asked. It was true, I hadn't thought much about Michelle's family up until then.

Sgt. Mulkin sat next to me with his arm around my shoulders and said, "Come on Joe. I know you're a good kid. These things happen. Let us help you."

"What do I have to do to prove to you guys that I'm telling the truth? Do you want me to take a lie detector test because I will? I'm not afraid because I'm telling the truth." I did not know what else I could do. This had gone on for hours. There was no other way I could prove to them that what I was saying was true. I was starting to feel I would be spending the rest of my life in jail for a crime I did not commit that has already ruined my life.

The investigators agreed that a lie detector test would be a good idea. Finally, they left me alone in the room one last time. I was now allowed to call my parents for the first time. My poor mother was in hysterics, and my father had an attorney on call. Dad was tough and felt he wasn't going to let anything happen to me. They believed in me, and both of them would have staked their lives on my innocence. Not just because I was their son, it was because they knew the type of person I was.

When I told Dad I was going to take the lie detector test he was upset with me. The attorney who had been speaking with my father and my Uncle John all morning advised against it. I started to cry on the phone. I was so scared and confused I did not know what to do, but my father's persistence had talked me out of it.

The door to the office I was in was open and across the hall I could see Leroy Anderson sitting in Sgt. Sullivan's office. He was calmly smoking a cigarette watching me talk on the phone. When we made eye contact he nodded his head to acknowledge me. He had a closed mouthed mischievous grin on his face. I was wondering why he was there and for a split second I was thinking about him and not myself. Why was he there? Did he see who had done this? Had they called him as a witness against me?

Just then Sgt. Mulkin came in to tell me the guy from the sheriff's department was there who would conduct the test. I had told my dad I would not take it before hanging up the phone. I told the

Sgt. that my father and I talked about it, and that I decided not to take the test because our attorney advised against it. This agitated him, but he felt it was best I speak with the test taker so I could make my own educated decision.

The guy who was conducting the test came into the room. He had been with the Monroe County Sheriff's department for years. He sat down across from me with his elbows resting on his knees. I told him I was nervous and I did not want my emotional state to affect the test. I knew enough about the test to know that what it measured was stress level, and at this point I can honestly say I have never been so nervous in my life. The officer reassured me that the machine would be adjusted to take my current stress into consideration, and then he said something I will never forget.

" I have been doing this a long time, and as I look at you I'm sure you did not do this. You look like a good kid. You have probably never been in trouble with the law in your life except for a traffic ticket or two. I know you want to know who has done this to your wife, and the police want to know too, but if they are spending two or three days running around trying to prove whether you did it or not that is time they aren't spending looking for the real killer. So, let's go and get you cleared so they can find out who really did this." Well that was it. Now I knew I had to take the test. I felt like he was on my side, and I believed what he told me.

I was escorted into the police captain's office where there was a long conference table. The officer started to hook me up to the machine. In the meantime, Sgt. Mulkin had gone downstairs where my parents, my Uncle John, and my two new lawyers where waiting for me. When the Sergeant told them I was taking the test my dad and mom hit the roof. Mom demanded that she be allowed to see me, but the Sergeant would not let her. "That's my son up there!" my mother shouted, as she made a bolt for the stairs, which led up to the office. Sgt. Mulkin stopped her and asked the officers that were with him to secure all the doors leading up the office.

Sgt. Mulkin looked straight at my father and said, "Your son is a big boy, and if he wants to take the test he will. But I know how you feel Mr. Forte. I have a son at home myself and I would do anything to protect him."

Back upstairs I was going through the questioning. I was asked a few obvious questions to help adjust the machine; like are my paints blue, and is today Thursday? These questions were used so he could judge my current pulse level to set the machine to only pick up dramatic fluctuations that would indicate a lie. Then the real questions began...

"Did you ever hurt your wife Michelle?"

"No" I answered.

"Have you ever hit Michelle?"

"No"

"Have you ever hit your sister?"

I paused... "No"

"Did you cut the phone lines in your apartment today?"

"No"

"Did you use a knife to threaten your wife at all?"

"No"

"Did you kill you wife Michelle Forte?"

"NO!"

When the questioning was over he took the report produced by the machine and left the room. I don't remember how long I was waiting, but it seemed like a long time. My body was still pretty hyper in spite of the fact that I had not slept all night. I had not even considered looking at my watch all night long either. It was as if time did not matter. I had no place to go, and I just did not care about anything. I just wanted to leave so I could see my family.

Just then the door opened and the testing officer walked in followed by Sgt. Mulkin. The officer looked at me with a smile shaking his head and said, "You were telling the truth." I felt a huge relief. Finally they believed me. Sgt. Mulkin held out his hand to me and we shook hands putting our free arms around each other's shoulders in a hug.

"I'm sorry we had to put you through all that Joe, but we had to be sure." the Sergeant said.

"I understand," I said as my eyes welled up with tears, " now go find the person who did this to my Michelle."

He looked me in the eyes with a closed lip smile and said, "We'll get um' Joe, we'll get um.'"

I was then lead downstairs to my family. When I saw my parents we hugged each other tightly and I said, "I passed the test, I passed."

My father shook the Sergeant's hand and thanked him. Sgt. Mulkin nodded to him and said, "We're going to get this guy, for him."

As soon as we stepped into the car the whole thing hit me. The shock of it all was gone, and now I was faced with the reality of what had all transpired over the past thirteen hours. It was now close to one p.m. and I was finally cleared. Just then I started to cry. I was left with the fact that Michelle was really dead. I had spent so long that morning just focusing on the dilemma I was in, I did not have the chance to take this all in. My life was changed forever, and I did not know what I would do.

CHAPTER 7

When someone you love dies suddenly it is like being punched in the stomach. First you don't know what hit you, and then you have to live with lingering pain. At that moment while I was driving home with my family nothing else in my life seemed to exist. I really didn't even know what to think, or how I should feel. All I can say to describe the feeling is I felt totally alone even when I was in a crowded room. I felt as if no one has ever felt this way, and no one could understand what I was going though. I was wrong.

We drove to my Aunt Natalie's house, which was only about three miles from the police station. My parents had been staying there since they left my neighbor's townhouse early that morning. My mother said we would be spending a few days there to avoid the press who by this time had already grabbed on to the story big time. I understand now, it must have been a good story for them. Young newlywed couple, murdered bride, husband being held for questioning, first murder in the Town of Greece in almost then years.... I had to face it, this was big news whether I liked it or not.

The next few weeks were going to be tough. I had no idea how tough they would be, but frankly, I had no expectations for a happy ending.

My Aunt's house was full. No one in my family had gone into work that day. My sister Theresa, my grandparents, Aunt Rita, Uncle John, and all the kids were there. I cannot remember being happier to see my family. The last thing I wanted at that moment was to be alone, and my family made sure I wouldn't be.

In retrospect my family was probably one of the biggest contributing factors to me getting through this whole mess. Without their love and support I would not have managed. I know it was tough for them those first few weeks to watch me in such pain, and I know that often times my mood greatly effected theirs. However, they always stuck by me, and I know they always will. My father has always told me that no matter what your family must always be the most important aspect of your life, because when all is said and done they will always be there for you. I feel so blessed to have such a loving and close knit extended family, but unfortunately not everyone does.

I could not believe it. All had gone so well for the two of us. How could it end now.... like this. You have got to be kidding me...I'm going to wake up from this right.... no, no this did not just happen.... I'll wake up, and all will be back to normal.... Maybe not.... This really did happen to you Joe.... Michelle is gone.... someone broke in my house and killed her.... for no reason.... AAAAAAAAAAAAHHHHHHHHHHHHHHHH. WHY GOD WHY HAS THIS HAPPENED TO ME?!?!?! WHY HAS SHE BEEN TAKEN AWAY FROM ME?!?!?!?! WHAT DID DO TO DESERVE THIS?!?!?! WHY, GOD, WHY, WHY why ...why.......why...........why.

I was just in plain shock, my family and friends were around me but it was as if everything was in slow motion. I could not understand what was going on. I was having pains in my chest; my heart was so heavy and broken. My emotional pain was so strong it soon became physical. I had never, ever experienced anything in my life that could have prepared me for this, unfortunately this would not be something that would go away soon. I depended on a lot of people now because I just could not do anything for myself.

Every time I closed my eyes I would see her. Not happy, smiling like she usually was, but lying there on the floor.... in our own bedroom in a blood soaked carpet.... dead. That scene was haunting. I could not escape it. That horrible terrifying vision was something I had no control over, please God make it STOP. All these feelings and thoughts as people would come over to see how I was holding up. People all around me, and I could not get this out of my head. The last thing I wanted was to be alone at this point. I was scared, scared to be alone. I have always preferred to be by myself when I was upset, but this was worse than anything I had ever felt before. I welcomed the sight of everyone.

Soon my mother-in-law came over, and it had been the very first time I had seen her since Michelle died. I'll never forget the look of absolute anguish on her face. My mother had met her in the kitchen and they embraced. Catina began to sob uncontrollably, she was finding it hard to catch her breath I think, but she managed to say these words that I will never forget. "I finally have my son, but now I've lost my daughter!" Those words were extremely painful to hear.

At the time I guess I was having a hard time seeing past my own grief, to notice the grief of those around me, but when I saw my dear mother-in law in such pain I wished I could take all of her grief upon myself. I had known Michelle for just over two years, but her mother had given birth to her, held her in her arms, and dried her tears. All the dreams she had for her daughter were horribly viciously destroyed in an instant for no reason what so ever. I felt sick for her, and again I began to cry.

She sat down beside me on the couch and we held hands. She was very concerned about how I was doing. She did not ask me any questions about what happened, but instead she just kept telling me that we needed to be strong for Michelle.

My friends Rick and Todd after hearing the news quickly caught flights to Rochester to be there for me. The guys, who had been there when Michelle and I met, were by my side right away. Both of them had moved away a year or so earlier. Rick was now living in Atlanta, Georgia, and Todd in Houston, Texas. When Rick arrived at my aunt's house it was all I could do to compose myself. He just grabbed and hugged me while I cried on his shoulder. They say a man who has one true friend in his life is truly blessed, so I guess I can call myself blessed twice over.

Then the news would come on. I had absolutely no idea how big this story had become, Michelle's murder was on every channel as the top story. My God, this cannot be happening. It was on at six p.m. and eleven p.m.; they would run promos during commercials, "the latest details about the Forte murder coming up at eleven p.m." Every channel ran the same thing. It was surreal as I sat watching the front of our duplex on television as coroners took my wife out of our front door in a plastic body bag. These things don't happen to people like me, only to drug dealers, and poor people in the inter-city. Not to me, or so I thought.

You might think after all I was going through emotionally that I would not be able to watch all this on the news, but I could. As a matter of fact I could not get enough. I watched every story on every channel that day just to see if I might learn something. Maybe these news reporters could teach me something that I did not know before, but they couldn't. I did not learn one new thing from the news I didn't already know. They talked about the kind of person Michelle was, the kind of person I was, the kind of neighbors we were, how Michelle was found, and that there were no suspects.

I would soon find out the person they really wanted to talk with was me. As if I could tell them something new, or show the people of Rochester just how I was doing. It would be quite some time before I would be willing to talk with them. For right now I was willing to let others do the talking for me.

I'll never forget one news report made the seemingly benign report that Michelle body was currently at the Monroe County Coroner's office, and I could not get the image out of my mind of her body lying on the autopsy table in a dark cold room. The vision of that was so painful. I cried out "My God, I don't want her to be there!"

Just then my father spoke up, "I'm going to talk with Falvo in the morning and get my daughter out of there." Falvo was of Falvo's Funeral home, which was the only undertaker any of my family had used since long before I was born. My father had also gone to school with the sons of Falvo Sr., "the old man" as my dad would call him. The sons were now in charge of the family business, and my father, as always, had someone he knew and trusted to handle things for us.

My father also had a very close friend from his childhood named Richie who sold caskets of all things. From what I understand most of the time he would only sell direct to funeral homes, but my dad called him to meet us at Falvo's the next morning.

There I was, twenty-four years old sitting in a funeral home with my parents and my mother-in-law, making funeral arrangements for my wife. I was a widower, this could not be happening. Michelle and I had not even gotten all our thank you cards mailed out from our wedding, and now I'm making plans for her funeral. As I sat there kind of in a daze, my father took over the situation.

"Richie", he said, "I want my son to get my daughter the best you got."

"This one right here Joe" Richie said addressing my father. Then he turned to me, "Joey don't worry about the price I'll do what ever I can for you."

The truth was I wasn't worried about the cost of anything at the time, or ever since for that matter. I agreed with my father. Only the best would do. It was the same situation at the cemetery. We chose to put Michelle in the mausoleum. My dad wanted her tomb to be eye level. Not on the floor or fifteen feet in the air, but right there as soon as you walked in. I agreed that we wanted only the best. The caretaker was showing us a map of the mausoleum with all the available tombs in the building. Each corridor was named after a Catholic saint. There was St. Mark's, St. Joseph and so on, but there was the perfect spot in the corridor named "Ave Maria". This was where Michelle needed to be. There was no other place that was as fitting as this. I'll never forget her singing that song with her mother. There were not too many things I was certain of in the last couple of days, but the fact that only the best would do for my Michelle, and placing her in the "Ave Maria" corridor were two things I was certain about.

At that time her mother and I had decided she would be laid to rest in her wedding gown. It had been such a short time ago that she was a bride and this was the way I always wanted to remember her. The morticians asked us to provide a scarf or a sachet, which could be placed around her neck to hide the fatal wound that opened up her throat. We were able to provide her wedding veil to be used for that purpose, a purpose for which it was never intended.

There are few things in life more painful then planning for the funeral of a loved one who dies unexpectedly. What did I know, all this was happening so fast? It was never anything we discussed ahead of time. Who would? We had just gotten married so the only plans we were making were for a family and a long happy life together. How did it come to this?

The wake itself was like a dream to me. I remember walking in the funeral home and into the parlor where she was laid out. As soon as we walked in I lost it. I began to cry uncontrollably. I don't remember who was holding me up, but there were two people, one on each side holding my arms to give me balance. I blacked out and fell to my knees. This was all way too much.

I was escorted up to the coffin that held my dear Michelle. I was having trouble breathing; every breath seemed to take tremendous effort. There she was lying there in her wedding gown. My beautiful bride just three months earlier, but now she didn't even look like herself. Her face no longer had the glow it used to. There was no shining smile or bright cheerful gleam in her eyes. This was the empty shell of my dear angel who had left her body behind some two days ago. I touched her hand and kissed her on the forehead then I had to sit down. My legs were very weak, and they were unable to support me.

I directed my family to retrieve a picture of Michelle we had taken last fall. I wanted the people who came to see her for the first time to remember her as she was, not as they would view her lifeless body now.

Soon our families' private time at the funeral home was over. Visitors started to arrive, and over the next couple of days they just kept coming. Over a two-day period Falvo's estimated that nearly five thousand people came by to pay their respects. I never thought we knew so many people. Friends I had in high school who I hadn't seen in years came up to hug me with tears rolling down their cheeks. Almost a dozen of my fraternity brothers I had back at the University of Buffalo. Old and current co-workers, customers from my FedEx route, priests and nuns from the many Catholic churches I and my extended family attend, friends Michelle preformed in plays with, her coworkers and friends, police officers, and people from the community we didn't even know came to tell me how Michelle's death had touched them deeply when they heard about it.

In my deepest sorrow, I had never felt so much love as I had then. God Bless them all, I can never thank those people enough for coming to show me their support and love, never. I don't think they could ever know how important it was for me to see each and every one of them. People stood in a line that went outside and down the block for an hour in the cold of February to see Michelle, her family and myself and show their loving support. I will never forget them. I can still remember the words of encouragement and individual conversations I had with many of them. I didn't realize it then, but here was when my family, friends, and many members of the community began to rally behind me to protect me.

The second day of Michelle's wake during one of the afternoon viewings, my Uncle John escorted me outside to get a breath of fresh air. The sun was shining bright and reflecting off the pure white snow. It was cold, but I couldn't tell. We watched the line of people waiting to get in go down the sidewalk and around the corner until you could not see the end. For the first time in three days I felt some peace, but it was for only a brief moment.

Then I looked across the street to see media cameras in the parking lot about one hundred yards away. Right then I was snapped back into the reality of what was going on around me. Uncle John asked me if I wanted to go in. I took a deep breath and we went back inside.

The next day it was time to lay Michelle to rest. We prepared to leave the funeral home early that morning. As my father had been so many times in the past he was our strength. He was the one who was there to witness when they closed Michelle's casket. He had to be sure everything was just right for Michelle and myself. Once again Todd and Rick stepped in as two of my pallbearers. They had been there when we met, the day we were married, and now finally the day we laid her to rest.

As the limousine my family and myself rode in left the parking lot of the funeral home, my mother noticed a FedEx truck parked across the street from the funeral home. The driver was Hank a longtime co-worker of my father and the driver who delivered in the mornings the same route I picked up at night. Hank looked at the limo and saluted us. It was quiet and somber. I watched out the back window of our limousine as a very long line of cars fell in behind us. Hank stayed until the whole procession passed him by.

We had her memorial service at Holy Spirit church. The church Michelle loved so much, and the priest, Father Bush, who Michelle admired so much. As we pulled in the church parking lot I could not help but to remember doing the same just three months earlier on our wedding day. Both days I pulled up to that church in a limousine over freshly fallen snow, and both days everyone was on hand to see Michelle and I. The irony was just too much. These two days were so close together in time the season hadn't even changed once yet. Just like the day of our wedding I would leave that church never to be the same again.

The inside of the church was packed with people. As I walked in I could see hundreds of people already there. Every seat was full and folks were standing along the walls just to be inside the sanctuary. Once again, as I had been at the funeral home, I was blessed to see so many people in attendance to show their support. My family sat in the front row. My mother sat on my left side holding onto my arm to let me know she was there. A priest who knew Michelle when he directed one of her plays in high school spoke so fondly of her outward love and enthusiasm for performing. It was a truly beautiful service and I know Michelle was pleased.

During one of the hymns, "Here I Am Lord", which I'm sure is talking of someone getting ready to die and ascend to heaven to answer God's call for him. Well right there, I almost lost conscientiousness. I became weak in the knees and had to sit down. I sat there leaning forward with my folded arms resting on the pew in front of me, and my head down as I began to sob so hard I was actually shaking.

As we were leaving the church I walked once again past all those who were there for me. Just as my family and I were heading out into the church foyer I was greeted by a row of my Federal Express co-workers as they stood together like military soldiers opening a way for me to pass through. When we left the church and preceded down the road to the cemetery I could see once again my company's presence. The street outside the church was lined with FedEx trucks of the drivers who were inside. Some who could not come inside were just pulled off to the side of the road to make sure I saw them as our limo drove by.

CHAPTER 8

In the days that followed the funeral the whole reality of facing life without Michelle began to set in. Up until this point everything seemed to be surreal. All the people and the events going on seemed to be like a very vivid dream that I could not wake up from. I had felt weak, but when everyone was around me I was guarded. Now, I was getting my first chance to be alone with my thoughts.

I moved back in with my parents after leaving my Aunt Natalie's house. The story in the media was beginning to die down and my mother and father thought it was okay for all of us to go home. I went back to the bedroom I grew up in. For so many years I came to this room as a kid to think about my life, and all the great things I used to dream I'd become when I finally got out of my parent's house. Now I was back. I remember being in such a rush to grow up through my teenage years, but now I really wished time would go backwards to when I was only sixteen years old again.

Right about this time my different emotions started to really surface. Mainly, fear and anger. Before now I was mainly in shock and probably a bit of denial. I was unable to sleep restfully I had horrible nightmares about the crime seen and being back in our apartment as someone was trying to break in. Mostly I dreamt Michelle was still alive, but in these dreams she would not talk to me. Sometimes her and I were still together, and other times Michelle was living back with her family and would not talk with me.

In one recurring dream I would call her house and her mother would answer. I was desperate to speak to her and to see her. All her mother would say is, "I'm sorry Joe, Michelle says she does not want to see you anymore, and she wants you to go on and forget about her.

In other dreams we would be at a public place and I would see her, and her eyes would meet with mine, and then she would turn away. I would yell for her, but she said nothing and would not acknowledge me. None of these dreams were ever pleasant. It was always me running or calling for Michelle, but she always just ignores me. Her face was missing that familiar bright smile and the twinkle was gone from her eyes. The same dreams would run over and over every night. It seemed as though they were always there, haunting me, mocking me. She was around me, close enough to touch but just out of reach.

I started to feel as if Michelle was communicating with me through my dreams, and the message I received was that she was upset with me. I felt I had let her down. I had always sworn to protect her, and I blew it. I wasn't able to save her. When I wasn't looking someone had taken her from me, and Michelle was very disappointed that I had let this happen.

At night I found it hard to fall asleep. I would stay up in the family room and just keep surfing the channels on the television never really able to settle on one show. I had to keep moving. Keep my mind alert. If I wasn't sleeping, then I wasn't dreaming and I could be awake to defend myself. At night in my bed I felt helpless and unable to defend myself from an attack. I didn't know who killed Michelle and why, but most of all I didn't know if they wanted to come back after me. This may be hard to understand... I was afraid of dying, but not afraid at all of being dead. I knew if I where dead I would be with her and this was something I wanted very much. However, the helpless feeling of being killed was very frightening and not something I wanted to go through if I could help it.

So, late at night I would sit up and would hear just about every noise possible that took place within a square mile of my parent's house. Most of the time I would stay up until I just passed out from exhaustion, and as soon as the sun came up I was up. This cycle was even worse then when I was a kid. Not since I was about seven years old, do I remember a time when the night had such control over me. I was so tired and emotionally drained, but I just could not sleep for fear of being off my guard.

When morning would come however, I was in complete control. This is when the anger started to show its face. I was alert and confidant and I felt the anger inside me could give me the strength of ten men. I wanted the murderer to come after me at these times because I wanted to take care of him myself with my bare hands. I was strong, confident and not afraid of anything. Then my emotions would go back down again.

I would spend a lot of time kneeled by the side of my bed in prayer, and I'm sure these prayers made absolutely no sense. At the start I would be meek and desperate, somewhere in the middle I would be sobbing, and by the end I would be pounding my fists against the mattress as hard as I could yelling.... WHYWHYWHY-WHY...WHO DID THIS TO HER!?!?!?!WHO?! Who?

Why and Who? I was consumed by these two questions and I wanted to do whatever it would take to find out the answers to these questions. Within a few days after the funeral I had made a couple trips to the police station to answer some questions for the investigation. I must have called those poor people everyday to ask if they had found out anything new. Sgt. Mulkin was always so patient with me. "We are working on it," he would say, "we are tracking down some leads."

Once I had gone to the police station to pick up some of Michelle's belonging, and while I was there I stopped to talk with Sgt. Sullivan. He wanted to just ask me a couple of back ground questions.

The Sgt. would say "Tell me again about Michelle's schedule.... how about this play she was in ... what was your contact with this Leroy Anderson?

"Leroy Anderson? What, my next door neighbor?" I asked, "He was just your typical always hanging around kind of pesky guy.... you know?"

"Well, was he ever upstairs in your bedroom?"

"In my bedroom.... no. He had been in my living room a few times I guess."

"Had you ever lent him your house key?"

I had to think a few seconds..."Yeah, one time I had him let in some furniture delivery guys."

"Do you remember if he gave the keys back to you?" he said.

"Yes, he left the key on the TV in the living room like I asked him to." I was starting to get very suspicious. "Are you looking at Leroy as a suspect?"

"Joe, we're still looking at a lot of different things right now. I want to show you a picture of a boot footprint. Do you recognize this print as the one you saw outside on the front porch of your apartment."

"Yeah, that's the one I was telling you about, do you think it may belong to the killer?"

"We don't know yet, we're just looking at everything."

On the way home I was thinking. Could it be Leroy? What would he do that for? How would he have gotten in our apartment? Sgt. Sullivan did say they were looking at a lot of different things, but Leroy.... we tried to help the guy out, why would he do something like this? I hope these guys know what they are doing.

When I went to sleep that night I had one of the most terrifying nightmares I ever had in my life. Michelle and I were back in our apartment upstairs in bed when we heard a loud noise downstairs in the basement. Michelle was petrified, she grabbed at my arm, but did not say a word, but I could tell by the look on her face she was more afraid then I had ever seen her in her life. I started to walk downstairs into the living room, which was filled with an eerie orange and red light. It was not the light you get from the sun, but it looked like the light that comes from the inside of a jack o' lantern at Halloween. The light was coming in from outside and illuminating the whole room.

I could see the shadow of someone outside on the porch, but something was telling me not to open the front door because the noise was still coming from the basement. It was a loud hollow dump like something was hitting the wooded stairs. I continued to move into the kitchen and opened the door to the basement. The light on the stairs was on, but I had to go down to turn it off because the switch was down stairs.

I got about three steps down the stairs and I heard the door slam behind me. Right at that moment I felt it. Something sharp was just plunged into my back, and I could feel my whole body go numb. Then I slowly turned around and there he was with an evil smile on his face that I can still see.... Leroy Anderson.

CHAPTER 9

March 10, 1993, just over two weeks had passed since Michelle's murder. Reality had settled in, and I was at the point where I was going to have to make some decisions about where my life was headed from this point forward. All the dreams and goals I had for Michelle and myself seemed useless to me now. I did not want to go back to my job at Federal Express in Rochester anymore. Even though I had enjoyed my job very much and looked forward to working with the company a very long time, the thought of getting back out on the road as a driver and continuing my management training course seemed very painful to me. I just could not bring myself to do it anymore.

That morning I knelt down by the side of my bed to pray for guidance. I could say for the first time in a while I tried to do more listening to God then talking. Finally after several minutes of prayer and meditation my direction was given to me. It did not come to me as a strange voice in my head from beyond or anything, but instead it was a moment of total enlightenment. When it hit me I knew in my heart that this was exactly what I was supposed to do, I had total faith that it was God telling me this. A peaceful feeling settled over me for the first time since Michelle's murder.

I was going to leave Rochester and move to Atlanta where I would complete my college education, because there was important work for me to do after my heart and mind where mended. My mother's sister and her husband lived in Atlanta as well as my best friend Rick and his fiancé Michelle, so I already had people I knew and loved there, which I felt was one of the most important things. I had already visited Atlanta twice and I knew there were many colleges there to choose from, and I was sure one of them would accept me. Federal Express would transfer me the same way they had transferred me before, so I would have a job when I got there. This time however, I would NOT let my job distract me from my education. I would work strictly part time, and devote myself to finishing my degree quickly and with the best grades possible.

That was it. This was what I was going to do. When I knelt down fifteen minutes earlier I did not have any idea what I was to do, but the moment I stood up I knew I could do nothing else.

A short time later some guests arrived at our house. Michelle's mother Catina and grandmother Grace came by to meet with a representative from the District Attorney's office division of Victims & Witness Assistance Program. Carol Mulhern was her name, and I didn't know it then, but she was going to be very supportive to us through the hard times we where about to experience.

We all sat down at the kitchen table, and I announced my plan of moving to Atlanta to everyone for the first time. My dear mother was understandably concerned. "Joey, honey it's too early to be making any big decisions."

"No Rosalie," Carol said, "getting away and moving on with his life is one of the best things he could do."

I understood my mother was nervous about me leaving. At this point she preferred that I would be right there where she could watch me. My mother also knew I had always been a strong willed person, but now was a time I think she needed me as much as I needed her.

Carol went on to explain to us about the process the police and district attorney were going through and some of the things we could expect would happen along the way. Not long after our conversation started, the phone rang and my mother answered it. The person on the other end was Captain Gomel from the Greece Police department. Mom listened intently on the phone as the whole room got real quiet. All of us were watching my mother talk on the phone, because even though I had been involved with the police in the investigation I was more often the one doing the calling and not the other way around. So, I figured this would be a break in the case. Suddenly my mother started to shout. "It was Leroy, it was Leroy!"

My God it was true, it was Leroy they had been investigating. I guess I can't say that I was really surprised, the questions the police had been asking me along the way made it clear he was a prime suspect, but now I knew for sure. What I didn't know was all the work the police had done to get to this point of being able to make an arrest. I was grateful the mystery of the whole thing was over because now I had a face to direct my anger towards.

All of us hurried to the living room to sit by the television where the normal broadcast morning was being interrupted for a special newsbreak. One of the local stations had a news crew on the scene as Leroy was arrested outside the welfare office in downtown Rochester. He was just leaving after picking up his check when the police grabbed him. He was put on the ground face down as police handcuffed him, and shackled his ankles. They then picked him up and put him into the back of an awaiting police vehicle. I watched this whole thing happen right before my eyes; literally just minutes after it had actually taken place. There he was the man who changed the course of my life forever in a single night.

I was to learn later from the police some of the things Anderson was saying to them during the arrest. What sticks in my mind the most is when Anderson was face down on the sidewalk; Sgt Sullivan was standing in front of him with his gun drawn. The Sergeant told Leroy he was "under arrest for the murder of Michelle Forte." Anderson just looked up at him and said, "I know."

The media had stepped back from the story after the first week, but this arrest was about to stir the pot once again. This time however, Michelle "the person" was now the "the murder victim" of Leroy Anderson. She had now officially become the backdrop to a murder, which was now the real story of the fate of Leroy Anderson. Everyone now wanted to know who this guy was. Up until this point any mention of his name by the police or the press simply did not exist. Now the true back ground to this story was about to unfold.

All day and into the evening the TV news was bringing new information to light regarding the life of Anderson and his very troubled past. Now, much more than before, I was learning from everything that was being said on the news, and now the police were much more willing to share what details they knew about him with me. I would soon learn the Leroy I knew was not the same man he made himself out to be. As a matter of fact, most everything he ever told me or anyone else in the neighborhood was a lie.

When we first met he told me the woman and children who lived with him were his wife and kids, but that was not true. He also said that he had a job with the county driving a snowplow. Well, he was getting a check from the government all right, but not for doing any work. He told others in the neighborhood about all the jobs he had including being a bouncer, and bodyguard for Michael Jackson. From some of the things I would learn later he pretty much told a different story to everyone he met, depending on what he thought would endear himself to them the most. I guess he used the truck-driving story with me because I was a truck driver. Maybe that was his way of gaining my trust, and it worked.

When this whole investigation started I would have never thought that Leroy would ever do such a thing. The police had found overwhelming evidence to the contrary. In his apartment they found his shoes, a shirt, and gloves that were stained with Michelle's blood. A key to our house was found on his key ring, and his fingerprints were all over Michelle's car, which by the way, he had stolen after the murder. DNA tests would later show some of his hair was left at the crime scene. Which may explain why from the time of the murder until his arrest he shaved his head bald. The police and the D.A. had built a really strong case against him with the evidence he left behind, but now it was time to go before a judge and prove it all.

CHAPTER 10

The media machine was now moving at full throttle. Coverage of the arrest had propelled the story back into the forefront, and I just like everyone else had to watch all that I could because the more I saw the more I learned about Anderson. I hardly knew this guy, and now, here he was being arrested for Michelle's murder. Two weeks earlier during my interrogation he was not even someone I would consider could have done such a thing. Then as the police investigation moved on it was no mystery to me they were looking at him pretty hard.

Why though? Why would this man who made himself out to be a friend do such a thing? The brutality of Michelle's murder itself would lead you to believe there was a lot of hate in this man, but for Michelle? Why? Why would you want to do this Leroy? What in the world was going through your mind? Maybe it was hatred against me, I don't know, but what I did know was I now had a name to fill in under my "WHO" question.

During the two weeks before Anderson was arrested reporters who were interested in interviewing me for the local news called me quite often, but I declined because I just did not feel comfortable opening up my life on the evening news at the time. I did not want to seek out the media in any way because I felt my grief needed to be private. Besides, after a few days there was no new information for this story, and I did not want my mourning to actually be the story. I just would not do it. In retrospect however, I do feel the local Rochester media was for the most part very respectful of my family and me. There were no reporters hanging outside my parent's home, so my privacy during this time remained intact.

There was one reporter Wendy Wright with the local NBC station who had called me a couple of times for an interview. I told her I was not ready yet, and that I had appreciated her understanding of my desire for privacy. I promised her I would be willing to give an interview as soon as a suspect was arrested as long as she continued to give me my space until that time. So, not long after Leroy was brought into the police station and away from the media cameras, I got a call from Wendy who asked if I was ready to talk to her. As I had promised, I agreed to give an interview.

Within an hour a media van was in our driveway ready to go. Wendy was not the reporter who showed up, but she sent a very nice young lady to do the interview for her while she stayed out in front of the police station. At first they said there would be enough time for them to get some footage and return to the station to edit and broadcast for the six o'clock news, but then they had decided it would be cutting it pretty close so they better do a live feed. Next thing you know the media van raises its thirty-foot antenna in our front yard, and the camera crew starts setting up my parent's living room like a television studio. This really intimidated me. I was going to go live on television. Under ordinary circumstances this would have been difficult, but the pressure I was under now I thought it would be almost impossible.

I do not remember much about the interview itself, except that I expressed my relief that a suspect had been placed under arrest, but I could not tell you any other questions I was asked or how I answered them. Later, I found out my interview was very important for some of Michelle's and my friends who had not seen me since the funeral. Many, I understand felt comforted that I was holding up okay.

Well the news that night on all the local stations was about Leroy the man, who he was, where he came from, and what the police and prosecutors were going to do to him now.

The police had been questioning him all day since his arrest between ten a.m. and eleven a.m., and it was now close to seven p.m. that night. It was now time for him to face a judge to be formally charged. One report was from the outside of the courthouse where some of Michelle's family members from her father's side waited outside the courthouse as they brought Anderson in for his arraignment. They were yelling at him, "God knows, Leroy! He knows what you did!" However, some of Anderson's family were there too and they were not about to let anything go unanswered, "God knows, you too!" they would say.

I really wished I could have been there at the time, but in retrospect it was for the best that I was not. It was nice to know that some of Michelle's family was there to show their anger and support. I did not know how bad it would get at that point, but I wanted desperately for the press to not forget about Michelle. However, I could see the focus start to shift to Leroy and the murder itself and not his victim, but that is the natural progression of things I learned. Once the victim is gone who is left to speak for her, except those who loved her? Now it was up to the police and prosecutor to see that justice is done.

As they were walking Anderson into the courthouse one reporter thrust a microphone in front of him to ask if he had committed this murder. Then it came out... "The only reason they have arrested me is because I'm a black man and an ex-convict." My heart sunk. Then I became filled with rage. Up until that point in all honesty, it had never even crossed my mind that Leroy was black, and it did not make a one bit of difference to me either.

All I wanted was the person who did this to be off the street. The "actual person" who did this, not the first black man police could lay their hands on. If the murderer had been a white guy I would have felt the exact same way because all I wanted was Michelle's killer brought to justice. When Anderson brought race into it the way he did, I was infuriated, but I was about to learn a very hard lesson because the race issue never went away. It would be the crutch Leroy would lean on to explain the situation he was in all the way through the process, and that angered me like you could not imagine. He was going to be judged based on a lot of very solid evidence and good police work, and that was all there was to it.

I had no idea at that time how long this whole process of justice would actually take, but I figured he would go to trial pretty quick and within the next two or three months he would be put away for life. Boy, was I wrong. Assistant District Attorney Richard Keenan was going to be the prosecutor in this case. I did not know it at the time, but he was called to the seen of the murder the night Michelle was killed, so he had been with this case before there was even a suspect. Mr. Keenan was very good to me through the whole ordeal, and he was always upfront with me. With him, just as with all the investigators at the Greece police department, he made me feel like I was a part of things. He would make me feel as if what I had to say was important to him and to the case. He was open and honest and I felt very confident Mr. Keenan would make sure justice was served in this case, but not only because it was his job but I felt a genuine sympathy in him that extended toward myself and Michelle's mother and family.

This was my first real life experience with the legal system and I depended on Mr. Keenan and Carol Mulhern from the District Attorney's office to help me understand the steps this procedure would have to go through. As you could imagine, when he told me the case could take a better part of a year to even get to trial I was crushed. I wanted so much for the whole process to be over quickly, so I could get on with my life. Mr. Keenan assured me things would all work out in the end, and I should not let the trial or anything else prevent me from moving on with my life. He too felt it was a good idea that I move to Atlanta to get away from the media and just leave everything to him and his office. So, when he gave me the okay to go I felt at that point there was little or nothing left to keep me back.

CHAPTER 11

I n early April things around home began to quiet down a bit. I had not returned to work at FedEx nor did I plan to before I moved to Atlanta. I guess I had made a connection in my mind between my life with Michelle and my career at FedEx, at least here in Rochester. It also didn't help that I was at work when the murder occurred, and I was unable to protect Michelle. The very thought of going back to my old position caused me a great deal of anxiety, and those I worked with and my managers were very supportive of me. The station manager Vinny, and my direct manager Scott worked very hard to ensure that my job stayed secure. They were in touch with the district managers and the Human Resources Department to help me with a transfer to Atlanta.

I made a preliminary visit to Atlanta that month to see how I would like living there. I stayed with my mother's sister Louisa and her husband David and son Christopher for two weeks, and I really enjoyed being away from Rochester. I felt at peace and able to let go a little. I slept much better when I was there, so I got some much-needed rest. Atlanta was where I wanted to be and where I believe God wanted me.

During my visit there I spent a lot of time with Rick and his fiancé Michelle. It was really ironic that both of us married women named Michelle, and it had been an on going joke between us before my Michelle's death. Rick and Michelle lived closer to the city than my aunt and uncle, and most of the colleges and universities that I was going to apply to were in the city limits. I was invited by Rick to live with them when the time came to make the move, and I accepted.

Meanwhile, as I was getting some much needed away time, back home my family and friends were moving all of Michelle's and my furniture out of our townhouse. I was so thankful for that. I never wanted to ever step foot in there again. The very thought of it scared me to death. I was told the carpet in our bedroom was removed all around the area where Michelle's body was found, and the place was covered with black fingerprint powder from the police investigation. From what I understand, most of the people who were there, my parents included, found the whole scene to be quite eerie and sad. Of course, not one thing was packed when they all arrived to move, but they were out of there in a matter of two to three hours with everything.

When I came back to Rochester after my trip to Atlanta, I started to go through all our stuff which was now stored in my parent's basement. I was looking for reminders of the life the two of us shared. I opened a box that had some of our kitchen supplies in it, and came across the ceramic vase that sat on our kitchen counter and held our cooking utensils. The outside of it was covered with the black fingerprint powder used by the police, and as I held it in my hand the realization hit me, there were policeman in our home investigating a murder. This was the same ceramic vase I saw a thousand times, and I even remember when Michelle bought it. She was so proud to be finally decorating her own kitchen, and this was one of the first things she ever bought. As I tried to wipe the black powder off the vase I started to cry. Why did this happen to me? What did I do to make it to this point in my life? How could anyone do this to us?

I finished going through our things and set up my room at mom and dad's house with all the things that gave me comfort. I kept the eight and a half by eleven-inch picture of Michelle that I displayed at her funeral on a table close to my bed. I set the table up like an alter to her. I had a few candles, her rosary, wedding garter, stuffed animals, and jewelry that belonged to her. I wanted to feel close to her, to feel her presence there with me. Every night I prayed in front of that table sitting cross-legged on my bed, in the dark with only the light of two candles on that alter. I would keep her rosary wrapped tightly around my left hand, and I was flipping through a Bible given to me by my sister with the other hand. There was an index in the back of the Bible, which listed common human struggles, and the Bible verses that pertained to them. There were topics such as "Experiencing the Death of a Loved one", and verses dealing with fear, depression and anger. All of which, provided me of short-term comfort.

God was not the only one from whom I was seeking any answers, but I was also starting to depend a great deal on New Age mysticism. A few years before I had even met Michelle, I developed a passing interest in the psychic world. Some friends of mine in college had turned me on to the excitement of it all. I started out using a Ouija board by myself, and then I moved to tarot cards, and automatic writing (when you hold a pen to paper and allow the pen to move by itself in answers to your questions). Originally this all started out as a passing fad that was fun, and I was able to get answers to whatever important questions I might have. It really was not a big deal to me. As a matter of fact I had put most of that stuff up the whole time Michelle and I were together. I may have done auto writing a few times, but for the most part I forgot about it.

Now, I had a whole new interest in it again a lot stronger then it had ever been before. I was very desperate and would try anything that might help me get a handle on things. I bought books on spirituality, talking with the dead, soul mates, meditation and even books about Hindu yogis. I had it all, and I was willing to see anyone or try anything that I thought might give me clear cut answers... to why this happened, was Michelle angry with me and is the pain ever going to go away.

I felt Michelle was angry with me and that I let this happen to her because I was not there to protect her. I did not listen to her when she told me she wanted to move from that townhouse, and all I had to do that day was call in sick like she wanted and she would still be alive. Better yet, maybe I would have been the one who was murdered and Michelle would still be alive. Guilt weighed very heavy on my heart, and I wanted to be sure Michelle was not angry with me, because I know I was very angry with myself.

In the dreams I would have of Michelle she would never speak to me, but only look at me a brief moment and turn away. I felt she was talking to me through my dreams and expressing her disappointment with me. Day and night these feelings were with me, and I felt I could only get my answers through psychics and my other new age methods.

God and prayer were good, but the answers just were not quick enough for me. Sure He pointed me in the direction of Atlanta, but I still had a bunch of things I needed to know right now. I did not have the patience to live on God's time, but I wanted him to live on my time.

There were two women psychics who I depended on a great deal during this time, and they had even become family friends. I knew they were trying to be as much help to me as they could. After my first couple visits they did not even charge me anymore. I'm sure I started to drive these poor women nuts after a while because I just kept calling them all the time, and asking the same questions over and over again. The whole thing started to become like a drug to me. Even if I got the answer I wanted I still kept asking the same questions to be sure. The more I asked the more I needed to know, and the more dependant I became on it. Never once during the next two plus years did I find anything wrong with my total reliance on mysticism.

Of course, I also tried other more conventional forms of psychotherapy. My Aunt Natalie recommended a psychiatrist to me who specialized in relaxation and visualization. This doctor helped me a lot by teaching me some of her methods, and above all she taught me that all the horrible things I was feeling were normal for someone who has gone through what I did. One of the most important questions I asked her was if she thought I would go crazy. I was very concerned I was going to just loose it, and become a lunatic in a straightjacket and rubber room. I had never had such strong negative feelings of suicide and anger like I was experiencing at this point. These were not feelings I had ever really felt so intensely before. I wasn't sure if my mind and body could take it all without just caving in.

My doctor would reassure me I would not go crazy because I was too strong to let myself go like that, and the fact that going crazy was actually something that concerned me proved that I was thinking sanely. Well, I had my doubts, but deep down I believed her and drew quite a bit of comfort from her confidence in me. Even though I felt in my heart she was right...I wasn't entirely convinced, and I always felt I was just one step away from the edge.

CHAPTER 12

June 12, 1993, three and a half months after Michelle was murdered I packed up a truck with my car hitched to the back to head to Atlanta. This was a very bittersweet day for me. On the one hand I was thankful to be getting out of Rochester and all the bad memories of the last few months, but I felt very intimidated about leaving my mother, father and sister behind. They helped me cope a great deal with the tragedy and I was not looking forward to living without them in the same house. I really needed them, but I also needed to leave town to regain the part of myself I lost. It was a tearful goodbye the night I left, but I knew my parents believed it was something I must do.

An old friend of mine, Mark drove down with me to keep me company and make sure I made it there safely. We had known each other since the fifth grade, and even shared an apartment together while I was going to school in Buffalo. We arrived in Atlanta late the following day after spending the night just outside of Cleveland, Ohio. It was a long trip and I was very tired, but when we arrived in town I caught a second wind. Excitement started to take over and I could not believe I was now going to be living in Atlanta, far away from all my troubles.

Here, I thought I could be anonymous again. I wanted people to know me for me, but I felt back in Rochester I would always be looked at by those I had never met as the "poor guy whose wife was murdered". I wanted to first be known as Joe Forte, good, honest, hard worker, who had something horrible happen in his life, but he did not let it get him down. In Atlanta, I did not have the media to spread the word of who I was. Back home when I would call to order a pizza, they heard about me. I went to the mall once with my sister and her fiancé just a week or so after Michelle died and a shoe store clerk looked at my credit card and said, "Forte? Hum, did you happen to know that girl...?"

I know people meant well, but I just needed a break. Just a chance to be free and get my self together. Atlanta gave me that perfect chance. Moving in with Rick and Michelle was a Godsend. I felt comfortable right away just like I was staying with family. This place was like paradise to me, and I was already starting to put my past behind me the first week.

When I started my new job at Federal Express I was actually looking forward to going back to work. It was nice to have something to get up for everyday, and the area in which I worked was unlike anything we had in Rochester. My position was that of a senior customer service agent behind the counter at a business service center. The office was located on the first floor of a trendy office building in the heart of one of Atlanta's business districts. It was a great place to work. The surrounding area was wooded with a large pond behind the building with a water fountain in the middle. I felt very comfortable and peaceful there, and the best part is it reminded me nothing of home.

The people I worked with were very nice too. I had a great manager who was very hands off and just let her people do their jobs, but when you needed her, she was available. My co-workers were also very gracious and welcomed me in with open arms. I had a lot of good friends there, and that is what I needed most.

I told myself before I started there that I was not going to tell anyone about what had happened to me. I wanted them to get to know me for me, and not feel sorry for me or be standoffish. One reason I came down here in the first place was to get away from the feeling that everyone felt they did not know what to say to me or have this pitiful look on their faces when they looked at me.

When I started there I wanted to have a clean slate. I was just the new guy in town. I wanted only to be known as a hard worker and student who came down here to finish school and move on from FedEx. So, that was just how it was. I thought that no one knew anything about me before I had arrived, but I was wrong. Apparently, a well meaning friend and co-worker in Rochester had told my new manager in Atlanta the very basics of what happened to my wife in hopes that it would ensure my new manger would "take good care of me". Had I known that the day I started, I would have been upset that my secret was out, but I did not learn about that conversation for over a year, and by the time I found out I was touched that my co-workers back home were so concerned about my well being.

Sometime in early July, I was notified that I had been accepted by Georgia State University located in downtown Atlanta. I was very excited, because now the plan was coming to life. I had a great place to live and work, and now I was going back to school. The best thing was, all of it was very easy. Everything was happening like it was meant to be. God had a hand in it I felt, and all the obstacles that may be in my way would not be able to stop me.

School did not start until the end of August, so I had a good six weeks or so to get used to working first before I would take on what would turn out to be a very tough schedule. My job did not start until three p.m. everyday, which gave me a lot of time for reading and lounging at the pool.

I often times found myself thinking about Michelle and all that had happened, but I would quickly push her out of my mind because every time I saw her in my mind it was on my bedroom floor covered in blood. My mind never naturally gave me flashbacks of any of the good times only the horror of that night, so I fought it...hard. I set up my bedroom, once again, as I had done in my room at my parent's house as a shrine to her. I hung the eight and a half by eleven-inch picture of Michelle over my bed, and my dressers were aligned with various knick- knacks and other things that belonged to her. I still wanted to feel her presence with me, but at the same time I did not want to entertain any bad thoughts of her in my mind.

Lorena, a dear friend of mine from back home came to visit me during those first few weeks in Atlanta. All I could talk about was how great it was down there, and how I was never going back to Rochester. She basically told me that I should not use Atlanta to run from my feelings, and that eventually I would be forced to deal with them head on. That had really ticked me off because I felt she did not want me to be happy, so I did not make the rest of her visit very pleasant I'm embarrassed to say.

However, I later learned she was right. Lorena was not trying to hurt me or stop me from feeling the pleasure I was enjoying in Atlanta, but she was trying to be a supportive friend. She knew all the excitement I was feeling would have a very short shelf life, and soon I would be forced to deal with the negative emotions I was hiding from here. I did not know it at the time of Lorena's visit, but things were about to get bad... real bad.

CHAPTER 13

On August 7, 1993, my new roommates Rick and Michelle were getting married back in Rochester. I had been away from home for less then two months, but already I had to make my first trip back. In a way I was looking forward to seeing my parents and family again. Things were going well for me up until that point, and I wanted my family to see I was getting along fine.

I was the best man in the wedding and I really wanted to show the support for Rick that he had shown me at my wedding and for me over the past few months. Sure, it was going to be hard to control my emotions, but it was something I had to do because people were depending on me. To make it even harder, my Michelle was asked to sing at the wedding by Rick and Michelle shortly after our wedding took place. She was excited too, because not only did she enjoy singing, Michelle also adored my friends and wanted to play a special part in their wedding.

I became engaged before Rick, and I remember my Michelle telling me, "Rick really needs to marry that girl." I'm not sure if it was the prospect of having other married friends she liked so much or what, but she was looking forward to this day even though she was never here with us to finally enjoy it.

The wedding went off beautifully. I admit I had a few difficult emotional moments, but there were plenty of people around to lend me support. One of the hardest moments I can remember was at the church. When Michelle was walking down the aisle I started having flashes of when my Michelle made that walk just nine months earlier. The sight of a bride walking down the aisle made me well up with tears. This was actually one of the first positive memories I had of Michelle and our time together since she died.

Now it wasn't that I did not want to enjoy pleasant memories of

Michelle, but the fact was that I couldn't. My mind would not let me get past the tragedy. I would have memories when I would lay in bed at night or during a quite moment alone just thinking of the good times we shared together when like a chain reaction one memory would trigger another so fast and it would always end up in the same place with Michelle dead on our bedroom floor. I wanted to stop that horrible image from coming to my mind so bad that I just fought every thought of Michelle that came to my mind.

All in all it was a good visit back home. The short time away did me a world of good, and I really missed my family and needed to see them. After the wedding, I flew back to Atlanta with Rick and Michelle, and the next night they left for their honeymoon, a week in the Bahamas. At first I looked forward to being alone for a while, but the first night would prove I was not quite ready.

I had not spent a night alone since Michelle died, and as I had said before, when I was asleep at night I felt vulnerable. Even though I was 1,200 miles from Rochester, and in a place I had considered paradise for the last few weeks, I was very anxious. I did not sleep hardly at all. I would stay up with the television and all the lights on until I literally passed out from exhaustion. Most nights I did not get to sleep before four or five a.m. It was a good thing I did not have to go into work until late afternoon, because after the sun came up I felt safe enough to get some rest. It was rough, and at the time I really was not sure I could ever get over the panic and fear I felt of being alone.

One of the nights that week I was reading in bed with the lights on at around eleven thirty p.m. when the phone rang. At first I jumped out of my skin because the phone never usually rang past nine p.m. When I picked up the phone beside my bed there was someone there but they did not respond when I said "hello". After about ten seconds of silence on the other end the person hung up the receiver. I knew someone was there listening to me, and my imagination started to run wild. I thought maybe someone was just checking if I was there by myself.

I jumped up and ran to the front door to be sure it was locked even though I had checked it several times that night. I was petrified, and I moved into the living room and turned on all the lights and the television. It was just a wrong number for Pete's sake. There wasn't anyone out to get me. Even though I kept telling myself this it was hard to convince myself it was true. I stayed up the whole night. When Rick and Michelle finally came home I was greatly relieved, but I never let on to them what the past week without them had been like.

The end of August brought the beginning of school. I was very excited and anxious to get started. Going back to college to finish my degree was the focal point of why I made the move to Atlanta in the first place. It would give me a purpose and goal in my life, which I so desperately needed to pull myself up from the despair I had been feeling. My degree would open up doors for me that could not be opened otherwise. I wanted to make a difference in society in a major way in some branch of government. I looked at going back to school as a period in which I would step back from the workforce and invest in myself. I was going to hit that school running and not stop or let anything distract me until I graduated.

I had more drive and ambition then ever before, because when I closed my eyes all I could see, was his face, and what he had done to ruin my life. At this time in my life I did not have a clear image of what I wanted to do after school was over, but I did know that whatever it was I wanted to be sure that Leroy and others who commit such destructive and evil crimes pay dearly.

Just like my friend Lorena had told me a few weeks earlier the novelty of living in Atlanta was really starting to wear off. After the first few weeks of school I started to feel it and understand what my true motivation was. The fuel that drove my mind and body was anger and hate for him. I pushed myself going to school from nine a.m. to two p.m. and then straight to work from three p.m. to nine p.m., twelve hours a day every weekday. Then I would get home by nine thirty p.m. and study until one or two a.m. and be up again by seven a.m. to start over again.

I was doing very well in school better then I had ever done before, and I was also a pretty good FedEx employee. I never let anything slip through the cracks. I became obsessive and a perfectionist, with very little patience for anything or anyone else that was not exhibiting the level of dedication that I was.

The problem was this fuel, my anger, that was driving me so hard to do and accomplish so much was also tearing up my body from the inside out. I never outwardly lost my temper in front of anyone for any reason, so all that built up hate, anger and hostility stayed bottled up inside me.

A few years earlier I was diagnosed with something called a spastic colon. What that means for me was during times of stress I would get a sharp pain in my stomach just below my rib cage on my right side. In years past it would act up during test time at school or other such pressure situations. It was not a severe pain, but it could be uncomfortable at times and would go away in a matter of minutes or hours depending.

The pain had also acted as a kind of forecaster to measure my stress level before a stressful situation even manifested itself. Sometimes the pain would come when there was nothing going on in my life that would indicate that I should be under stress. It was as if my body was reacting to stress before the situation even occurred.

However, after a couple of years of having it under control, it now came back with a vengeance lasting for days or weeks at a time. The level of the pain was often triple what it used to be. It went from a mild discomfort to sometimes doubling me over with sharp attacks of pain. It felt like a knife was piercing my side at times, and other times it felt as if someone had their hand around my colon and they were squeezing it as hard as they could.

After going through two or three weeks of this I decided to return to psychiatric counseling. I needed to be able to talk freely about the rage and hate I was feeling. I would have liked to talk with family or friends, but I was afraid if they heard about the feelings and thoughts inside me it might cause them to become very worried about me. I figured talking with a professional who happened to be a stranger might help me to at least pull the cork and let some of my hostility escape.

Well, I went to a psychiatrist for two or three visits. At first, of course, I had to give him the background story of Michelle's murder. Then I went into the daily emotions I was feeling that were eating away at my insides. I remember telling him I had violent daydreams of going into prison where Leroy was and killing him with my bare hands. I fantasized elaborate plans on how I could be sent to prison just to be able to get to him. It did not matter that he was twice my size because my anger would take over and he would not stand a chance. I thought of all kinds of ways to do him in and the scary thing was I was enjoying those thoughts a bit too much for my own liking. I wanted these thoughts to stop along with the pain in my stomach.

After listening to me spout off for a couple of visits the doctor finally suggested that maybe I should take some medication that would help me control my anger a bit. TIME OUT! No way. I did not want to take anything that I may somehow become dependant on. Sure, I could have used something now and then that would calm me down, but I wanted to learn how to work through it myself without taking anything that might just mask the problem instead of dealing with it head on. I realized that prescription drugs can be helpful in a lot of cases, but this was just one road I did not want to go down. Frankly, I feared prescription drugs because in the state I was in, I felt I could easily become addicted. So, that was my last visit to him and I have never gotten any other counseling since then.

Just about that time, as my mind was becoming more active my body was staging a revolt. By late September I became physically sick. It started out as a cold and quickly developed into bronchitis. I'm sure a big part of it was the change in weather from summer to fall in a different climate from Rochester, but my body just could not kick it. I could not shake this hard, sometimes violent, cough for over three months. My cough did not completely go away until early January. One night as I was sleeping, I woke up suffering from a violent cough jag that was so hard I actually slightly tore my sternum from my chest bone.

Over the span of three or four months I lost thirty pounds. I went from a healthy one hundred seventy-five pounds to a sickly one hundred forty-five pounds, and at five feet ten inches one hundred forty-five pounds made me look pretty sickly. I did not eat much and slept even less, so I wasn't giving my body a chance to build back strength.

Even through all that, I refused to miss even one day of school, and I only missed a couple days of work after my sternum tore.

There were many times I would have to excuse myself from class because I would start coughing so hard I could not catch my breath. That never stopped me though. I kept the same frantic schedule that whole time.

Now I don't know for sure why I became sick, and why it took me so long to shake it. I had been sick before, but rarely had it ever gone on greater than two weeks. It was very self-destructive I know, but I guess that was what I was trying to accomplish. Either I was going to succeed or die trying and it did not matter to me which.

CHAPTER 14

Guilt is a very powerful emotion. It can drive you to run away, and at the same time it can eat you from the inside out until you just explode. I tried my best to distract myself from it and push it out of my mind while at the same time trying my best to hide it from the people around me.

The type of guilt I felt made me constantly second guess almost all the decisions I had made leading up to the point of Michelle's murder. I wished I would have listened to her when she told me a few times that she felt afraid and uncomfortable and wanted us to move. I thought she was imagining things and I wasn't about to move after only four or five months. Michelle would tell me Leroy made her nervous, and all I would say was that he was just a harmless pest. I just did not listen to her or take her fears as a serious threat. It was my fault for not taking her from that situation and I would beat myself up about that fact often.

Michelle looked at me as a protector, but I wasn't there for her when she needed me. I worked nights and I would leave her home alone, vulnerable. How could I have done that? I knew she felt scared, but I wasn't there for her. The one real job I had was to comfort her and make her feel secure, but I failed. While I was away... I lost her. I let her down.

Many times I would I wish we had never married or even met, because at least then she would have still been alive. I loved her so much, that if I was given a second chance and I knew the future of what would happen to her on that snowy cold winter's night, I would have never taken her from her grandparent's home. To me it would have been better to never enjoy the pleasures of having Michelle enter my life in the first place, as long as she would have had the opportunity to live a full life to a ripe old age. It was my fault. I put her in that situation, and I did not listen to her when she asked me if we could leave.

The overwhelming feeling I had was that Michelle was upset with me. Not then, but now. Her spirit would still come to me in my dreams, and the reason she would not talk with me was because she was angry with me. I would constantly play with those tarot cards over and over again. I wanted to get a message from her. I needed to know she was okay and was not angry with me. I would just keep shuffling those cards until they told me what I wanted to hear. Sometimes spending hours.... shuffling.... dealing.... and reading those cards. I would call out to Michelle because I wanted to hear from her, but she never came.

So, that was the pattern I lived with. Fear, anger, and guilt. I went from one to the other over and over again in my mind while those feelings were slowly tearing me apart from the inside out. During this whole time the shadow of Leroy's trial was looming over my head. I felt like he was taunting me by not letting me move past this emotional cycle. I knew I had no chance of putting everything behind me and trying to heal myself, when something so huge still lay ahead of me. I almost tried to rationalize it with myself. I figured why even try to make strides emotionally when the upcoming trial will only destroy any progress I would make.

Back in Rochester the prosecution and Leroy's defense were going through pretrial motions. These were requests that the defense attorney would file with the judge to get evidence removed from trial or even to have the whole case thrown out and allow Leroy to walk free. Well, each time a motion was filed with the court it would merit a small news story on the six or eleven o'clock news, and even a short story in the local newspaper. My mother, God bless her, would call to tell me each time one of these stories appeared. She tried to keep them from me, but I would coax her to tell me if anything was going on. In reality these pretrial motions upset my mother a great deal too, and I think she wanted to vent her frustration to me over what we thought was ridiculous.

Leroy's attorney succeeded in actually getting what I felt were some key pieces of evidence removed from the trial. For instance, his key ring had a copy of Michelle's and my house key on it, and I assure you it was not because we gave it to him. There were two occasions when we let Leroy borrow our keys for an extended period of time. Once back in late December I was working overtime in the early morning at FedEx because of the Christmas rush, and I asked him to let in furniture delivery guys while Michelle and I were at work. He had the house key to himself almost all day. Of course the other time was when he borrowed the car, that was the night he was pounding on the front door, and Michelle called the police. Michelle gave him her whole key ring, which included our house key.

This piece of evidence was huge in my mind, because it explained how he was able to get in without a forced entry. Now it was thrown out because it wasn't an item on the search warrant the police obtained for Leroy's apartment, so it was thrown out and the prosecutor could not use it at trial as evidence.

Well, needless to say successes like this in Leroy's defense would set me off big time. I really did not know the whole give and take of the criminal law process at this point, and I felt any victory for him would destroy the case. I was a nervous wreck, and angry every time I would hear about any of these things.

The pressure and stress from all this were really getting to me, and a few times at night while driving home from work I thought, "ya know.... if I drive up under this tractor trailer here at 90 mph, it could all be over right now. Forget about all this, and just get out of here to be with my Michelle." Then I would think of what that would do to my mother and father. I would break their hearts, and for some reason I felt I would also break Michelle's heart too for not staying back and seeing this through until the end. So, I could never do it. There were things I knew I had to do here, and besides if I killed myself the only real winner would be Leroy himself. Then I vowed never to let him defeat me by controlling my emotions.

CHAPTER 15

By mid-October I was thoroughly entrenched within my negative emotions, and only the distraction of school and the constant companionship of Rick and Michelle kept me on the straight and narrow. Believe me, there many moments I just wanted to drop out of society and disappear leaving all this behind me, but I couldn't, too many people would be hurt if I did. My family and friends were very important to me and somehow I sensed that if I portrayed an image that I felt good to them, they felt good and vise versa. So, I was very careful how I acted around everyone.

By now I really needed some comfort by my parents back home, and I was about to have the perfect excuse to travel back to Rochester to see all my family. My Aunt Natalie was getting married on October 15th back home and I would not miss it.

Before I left of course I was only thinking of the positive feelings this union would bring about. I figured that I had a good time at Rick and Michelle's wedding this one should be even better because all my family would be there instead of just my parents and sister. Well, I was about to find out there was a very real negative side to that. You see, emotionally I was at a breaking point because I held in and repressed all my feelings for so long I was due for a melt down.

It came while at the church during the service when the singer at the church began to sing Ave Maria. The voice could not have been anymore familiar to me because the singer was none other then my mother-in-law Catina. The tears began to over take me. I had not cried like that since Michelle's funeral. Finally after so long, I was having the beautiful memories of Michelle without reverting back to the terrifying thoughts of the night she died.

In every note Catina sang I could hear the echo of her beloved daughter's beautiful voice along side hers. I was overwhelmed, and I cried so hard I began to shake and my knees became weak. My mother, standing next to me, also had tears in her eyes, and as I looked up I could see everyone was looking at me sharing in my grief. My father, sister Theresa and her fiancé Mike, my Aunt Rita, and Uncle John, and my grandmother were all crying. My Aunt Natalie and Larry even looked down at me from the alter with tears in their eyes.

That moment when everyone was crying with me did something to me that nothing else any one of them had ever said to me could have. I felt such an unbreakable bond with my family right then that words could never express. No matter what, they would be there for me we were connected...we are family.

There are a few words of wisdom my father has bestowed upon me in my life that are always in the back of my mind. He would say, "Most people in your life come and go, but your family will always be there for you. Family needs to stick together always no matter what." He was right, regardless of all that had happened to me I truly believed I was blessed with one of the best families ever, and I thank God for them all.

After the ceremony my mother-in-law and I had a very tearful and hugging reunion. I was truly glad to see her and we engaged in some standard small talk about what I was doing, how things were going. It was nice. My aunt had told me ahead of time Catina would be singing at the wedding, but I thought it would be just fine. I had no idea it would provoke such strong memories and feelings out of me, but I'm very glad it did. Those tears were just the emotional release I needed.

That night at the reception I packed all those emotions back deep inside me, and I found getting drunk helped the packing go smoother. It wasn't the first time and it certainly would not be the last.

CHAPTER 16

Going home for my aunt's wedding to see all my family and to just have a good cry was just what I needed at the time, and seeing Michelle's mother again made me feel close to Michelle. When I went back to Atlanta I felt somewhat refreshed. I was hoping to hang on to that feeling another six weeks or so until final exams.

School this time was very different for me. I was just going everyday doing my thing, studying in the library and going to work. I was treating my classes now like they were my first job. I was on a mission, and Georgia State was the perfect place for me.

The university was made up of mostly commuters so there were few of the on campus temptations that were in dorm life. Lets face it, anyone willing to battle Atlanta rush hour traffic everyday to attend college downtown is a serious student. A lot of the students I met were like me because they were either going back to school after leaving in their youth, or just starting later. At twenty-five years old I was a bit on the young side with regard to my fellow students.

The first quarter I took Constitutional Law, Judicial Process and Legislative Government. I really wanted to get a feel for the judicial system, and I craved any knowledge I could get. I really did enjoy those classes, but none of them discussed the criminal process of the legal system, which is really what I wanted.

My professor for Judicial Process, Dr. Thomas, who later that quarter became my academic advisor, was a great help to me. Only a couple of weeks into the quarter I went to talk to him after his lecture. He was one of the first people in Atlanta I confided in about all that had happened back home. I even brought in newspaper clippings that would help me explain some of the things I was still a bit uncomfortable talking about.

I told him the current stages of the legal process we were going through, and he explained to me some things I could expect along the way. I felt Dr. Thomas was an important ally for me because I really needed someone knowledgeable who could help me understand the process as it was taking place.

I knew the trial was going to take place sometime next winter in the middle of the next school quarter, so I was thinking of taking it off. Dr. Thomas however talked me out of it, he said you can never be sure when the actual trial is going to take place, and the distraction of school may help me to keep my mind off of things. He was right. I wasn't going to stop now, I needed to get on with my life and not let Leroy's trial stop me from doing what I needed to do. So, I took his advice. I was going to keep on going until I finished.

The week after Thanksgiving brought an end to that first quarter. I ended up with one A and two B's. Which was my best academic performance since my freshman year at Kent State. All in all it was a good feeling to have done that well at three of the hardest classes I ever took with all that my emotions were putting me through. After I made that first hurdle and proved I could do it I had an even stronger sense of purpose.

December 5th, the day that would have been Michelle's and my first wedding anniversary, and it was a very hard day to get through emotionally. Rick and Michelle had tried to keep my mind busy that day so that I would not let myself get too down, but I could not help it. I ended up drunk late that night, and in my room rummaging through a trunk I had put together with all of the things that had meant so much to Michelle and I. There were pictures, cards, love letters and small gifts we had exchanged over the course of our time together.

I had not been in that trunk since I put everything in it before moving to Atlanta. I held tightly to the words Michelle would express to me in letters she had written to me when I was in Buffalo and she in Rochester. I could hear her in my heart saying the words to me that were written in those letters. I spent a great deal of that time wishing she was there with me to share our first anniversary. That was the way it was supposed to be for young couples to spend a romantic first anniversary together remembering the excitement and beauty of their wedding day while looking forward to the many happy years yet to come.

Well, things just did not work out that way for us, and all I could think of was, why wasn't Michelle here with me? What is it that I had done in my life that made me deserve to have my wife taken away from me so soon after we had begun our life together. Why was I spending what should have been one of the most romantic nights of my life drunk, holding on to pictures of my wife instead of holding her. How was I supposed to make it through all of this without losing my soul and my mind, and who cares if I live or die?

I passed out, and woke a few hours later on the floor still in the same spot with all the things from that trunk spread out around me.

Chapter 17

Somehow, I survived the holidays, but in all honesty I can't remember too much about them. Of course I went back to Rochester for Christmas making that my third trip back in a six-month period. Although it was a good thing for me to be away I could never cut the cord completely. I felt I needed a place to go back to that was waiting for me. My parents left my room as I had the last day I was there, and I always felt a peace and sense of belonging when I was in my parent's house.

However, I still felt that I would never go back to live in Rochester ever again. Sure, I got the big welcome when I came back from all my family and friends, but I knew if I was living there everyone including myself would have their own things to do and I would be forced to deal with everything all over again.

Back in Atlanta the New Year brought a new quarter of school and the uncertainty of Leroy's pending trial date. I hoped in my heart the trial itself would never take place because the thought of being there brought on extreme panic and anger. As Dr. Thomas had advised me I did not take off that quarter of school, because I was worried a break would destroy the momentum I had built up. If the trial was put off a month or two it could not only waste that quarter but the spring and summer quarters too. Besides, I needed something to distract me otherwise I could spend much of the coming months with nothing to do but worry.

As February approached it looked as though the trial was going to take place that month. Not only was I going to be in attendance, but I was also one of the prosecution's witnesses. Even though my testimony would not be one of an eyewitness, it would allow the prosecutor to lay a foundation of who Michelle Lentine-Forte was and what our dealings with the defendant were like.

Although I was scared, I did look forward to the chance to help the prosecutor and the police send Leroy to jail. It was the same sort of feeling I had early in the investigation when I was able to help the police with little things here and there. The trial was going to be my way of helping avenge Michelle's death, and this was very important to me.

The second week of February 1994, the trial was set to begin. Right from the get go controversy over the jury selection caused an uproar from the defense and some local black leaders once again brought the issue of race to the forefront. Even the famous Rev. Al Sharpton all the way from New York City would became interested in poor Leroy's plight, because the jury selected for the trial did not contain any African-Americans. The jury would come to be known as the "all white jury".

The original jury pool contained only three African-Americans who for one reason or another were dismissed. Rochester's African-American population is not that large to begin with; I believe it to be somewhere around 10%-15% of the general population. Further the pool from which potential jurors are selected comes from a list of eligible voters, so anyone who is not registered to vote in Monroe County will not even be called to serve. At the time I don't even believe that half of my family was registered to vote, so to me the race issue was infuriating.

However, all that aside, the thing that burned me most about the entire situation was that it was insinuated that an "all white jury" was not capable of hearing all the facts and rendering a fair and unbiased verdict when an African-American defendant was involved. To me I did not care one bit what the color of Leroy's skin was. It didn't matter when we tried to help him and his family by being good neighbors and it certainly did not matter to me now. If Leroy had been white it would not have changed the anger and hatred I felt toward him at all. To tell you the truth I wish he was white, so that the race issue would not have even played a part in the whole thing.

As testimony in the trial was about to begin the whole "all white jury" controversy took a back seat to the proceedings themselves. Although the issue was never brought up again formally, we definitely had not heard the last of it.

The trial began the second week of February 1994, almost a whole year since Michelle was murdered. I was of course up in Rochester from the start. The D.A. was planning on calling me as a witness the first day. My testimony was primarily to lay some groundwork for the prosecution's case. Frankly, the only evidence I knew of that would link Leroy to the crime was told to me by the police.

The first day I was told to arrive at the courthouse early. Richard Keenan the D.A. was not sure how soon they would be calling me, but he had me down as the third or fourth witness. I was not allowed to be in the courtroom while the first few witnesses before me were giving their testimony because there could be no sign that the testimony of the other witnesses would affect mine. Further, the D.A. believed if I was in the courtroom, as a future witness, and as the victim's husband, my very presence could influence the jury. Either they would be looking at me to see my reactions to what was being said, or they just may draw an opinion of me before I had a chance to testify.

During the time that the first witnesses were in the courtroom I stayed in the D.A.'s office, and in the waiting room outside the Victim's & Witness Assistance office. I tell you... I was a nervous wreck. Scared to death. I did not want to do or say anything that would jeopardize the case. I was really afraid of having the attorney twist and turn my words around like the police officers did on that first night. I did not like that helpless feeling one bit of being unable to convince someone who did not believe me. This time I was in a room full of people and the jury, so I did not want to relive that again. Richard Keenan the D.A. assured me that if any badgering was going on he would "object", and he also told me that juries do not look fondly on defense attorneys who treat victims as if they were the criminals.

This would also be the first time I would see Leroy face to face since the time we were in the police station that first night. I had to keep thinking to myself that I wasn't the one on trial and God would help me through this. I went to his arraignment last spring, but I was sitting in the gallery and his back was to me so we never made eye contact with each other. I was not sure how I was going to react, or how he would react. I was hoping he would be too intimidated to look me in the eye after what he had done.

So, after sitting in the waiting room for hours not knowing how things were going in the courtroom all of a sudden Mr. Keenan came in followed by my parents and members of Michelle's and my family. I was informed calmly by him that the defense had demanded a mistrial, and now court was adjourned until tomorrow when the judge would render a verdict of whether a mistrial was warranted or not. Oh no! What happened in there? I was now in full panic mode, and once again my heart sunk to my stomach.

During the questioning of one of the police investigators who worked the case Mr. Keenan asked her if she could recall a conversation she had with Leroy prior to his arrest. The investigator repeated parts of a conversation, which related to Leroy's employment and so forth. Then she was asked if he told her anything else, and the she said, "Yes, in relation to that also, he told me he was the subject of a police murder investigation."

The defense attorney jumped up and immediately objected, and the judge sustained and had the jury excused. The defense attorney made a motion for a mistrial claiming prosecutorial misconduct. The defense felt any mention of involvement in a prior crime could bias the jury. Mr. Keenan argued that it was an innocent statement made by the investigator, and the statement was not equivalent to the admission of a prior crime. Besides the defense had a copy of the investigator's police report and never moved to strike the statement at any of the pretrial hearings.

After the judge listened to both sides he dismissed everyone so he could have the night to research his decision. Mr. Keenan informed us if there were a mistrial the whole process would have to start over again with a new jury. With this being the first day of the trial not all would be lost if a mistrial were declared, maybe a week or two, but worst possible case the trail may have to be put back on the calendar and be delayed weeks or months. Lord, I did not want that to happen. After all the gearing up emotionally for the trial it would have put me in knots to have the trial postponed.

Everyone was told to go home that night and not to worry. It would not be until morning when the judge would make his decision. There was of course nothing anyone could do at this point it was up to the Judge (Donald Mark) to make his decision. My family, Michelle's family and myself were instructed to come back in the morning prepared to continue the trial, and we would just have to see how the judge would decide.

"Don't worry," he says. Yeah right I thought. We have waited a year for this trial to take place, and now there was a possibility that it may be declared a mistrial and lost somewhere on the long court docket. I was sick to my stomach all night. Because no matter how the judge decides either this trial is scraped or I go on the witness stand, both of these case scenarios had me ill.

The next morning came and with it came Judge Mark's decision not to declare a mistrial. The decision was of course not based on his own opinion, but an extensive case law report he had done the night before. In short the trial would go on and the jury would be instructed to disregard the witness' statement.

I was not in the courtroom at the time because as I said earlier I could not go in before my testimony was given. Carol Mulhern with Victims Assistance came out to the hallway where I was sitting outside the courtroom to inform me of the good news. We were still on and I was going to be the next witness called after the police investigator finished up her testimony from the prior day.

Back in the waiting room of the D.A.'s office my Uncle John stayed to keep me company while the rest of my family was in the courtroom. I was grateful for him being there. His level headedness kept me strong at the funeral and now he was here for me again at the trial.

Carol Mulhern came out to tell me I was the next one to appear on the witness stand, and my heart started beating through me chest. "Here we go" I thought, "I need to be strong for my Michelle. Here is where we get him honey."

I was led into the packed courtroom as everyone turned to watch me walk in. I didn't know how to react to all this attention, so I just walked looking straight ahead to the witness stand, my final destination, where the assistant D.A. Richard Keenan was waiting for me. As I walked through the gallery and into the area where the attorney and defendant sat, I saw Leroy and he saw me for the first time in almost a year. Our eyes locked as he stared at me and I at him. I passed by his table and to the witness stand and turned to give the oath. When I sat back down Leroy and I resumed our staring contest.

As I looked at him I saw ... nothing, he had absolutely no expression on his face, just a blank cold stare. I expected anger or maybe even fear; at least I hoped I would see fear, but there was nothing. Cold, blank nothing of a look almost as if he were staring into space and just happened to be looking in my direction at the time.

I remember thinking I can't believe this guy has the nerve to look me in the eye, and without even an ounce of emotion. I know my eyebrows were getting tight as they dropped, and I was struggling to fight back a snarl on my lips. I had a Clint Eastwood face on like I was preparing for a gunfight. Yet he was giving me no such emotion in return, and that was making me extremely angry.

I know I answered the prosecutor's first few introductory questions without even looking at him. I just kept staring at Leroy trying to get him to give me a reason to jump off the stand and run over there to break his neck. You may have noticed at this point I was not even the slightest bit nervous, but instead I was filled with anger towards this man. I soon came back into my right mind and realized Mr. Keenan wanted me to look at him and the jury not Leroy. So, I gradually shifted my attention toward them, but I was keeping an eye on Leroy who did not change one thing about his look.

The questions the prosecutor was asking me helped put me at ease after a while. He was trying to have the jury get a clear picture of who I was and who Michelle was. He asked about our relationship, how much I loved her, what was I doing now, and what was I studying. Then he started getting into the more important questions of evidence identification, and then I could feel myself move into the same frame of mind that I was in a year earlier on my many trips to the police station to help with the investigation. I knew what I was doing was an important part in the case and I took it very seriously. It was as if the room was now empty and I was just talking one on one with Mr. Keenan.

I was asked to identify my purple bathrobe, which was found

downstairs in our basement. I also identified Michelle's snow brush which we kept in her car to clean the windows, and finally I was asked if I could hear the water running in Leroy's apartment when they were taking a shower next door, and the answer was "yes.' All in all Mr. Keenan did not keep me long, but just long enough to lay the ground work for some evidence he would introduce later on. By the time he was done I felt pretty good. I was strong and confident, and I knew I did the best I could and Michelle would be proud of me.

However, all that would soon change quickly as I was about to under go cross- examination by the defense attorney (whose name by the way I remember, but I will not use. Instead I shall refer to him only as the defense attorney or Leroy's attorney.) Anyway, as soon as he started in I could figure out right where he was heading with his defense.

The first question I was asked was how big was Michelle, for which I answered about five feet tall, one hundred twenty-five to one hundred thirty pounds. The defense attorney then had a smirk on his face like he caught me in a lie. Then he walked over to his table and picked up a report to bring over to me. It was the autopsy report from the coroner. When he asked me to read aloud what it said under height and weight.

" Five feet, three inches tall, and one hundred fifty-five pounds" I read.

" So what do you have to say about that" he replied.

" I don't care what this report says I know how big my wife was and she wasn't that big."

He came up to me only slightly defeated to take his report back and he tossed it back on his desk from a few feet away. He then grabbed a picture from his desk and asked me to identify it. When he brought it to me I looked at it a second and answered, "These are my car keys." The police took the picture of my set of keys, which I dropped in the bedroom just a few feet away from Michelle's body that night.

" Mr. Forte," he began, " can you locate anywhere on that set of keys in the picture, the keys to your Pontiac Grand Am?"

I looked a second or two, and answered, "Yes."

I could tell by his reaction right away that was not the answer he expected. "Where do you see them?"

"Right here." I said pointing to them. He looked, and I think for the first time he saw them too. He snatched the picture away and went back to his table to regroup.

All the while I'm thinking you have got to be kidding me. I could not believe he was asking what were to me ridiculous questions that I felt could not be helping or hurting Leroy, but I tell you this line of questioning was certainly making me feel more confident. Bring it on, I thought.

Then one of the strangest things happened in the courthouse, the fire alarm went off about an hour into my testimony. We were all ordered to leave the building for the drill. When I came down off the stand Leroy was only about ten feet in front of me. He had his back turned and was talking to his family. Two police officers stood at his side and had his hands cuffed behind him. At that moment all I could picture myself doing was jumping on him and breaking his neck with my bare hands. All this would be over and I will have gotten my revenge. Just then Mr. Keenan walked up to me and said I should stick with him outside. I would never have attacked Leroy there, but I sure felt like I could have, and should have killed him right then and there.

While we were outside Mr. Keenan told me what a good job I was doing up there by not letting the defense trip me up. It was as though I knew where he was going with a question before he did. The questions were not meant to stand alone, but the defense would build on each of my answers to trap me in the end. However, each path he tried to lead me down I brought him to a dead end. Because basically he had nothing and he could not fight against the truth.

Mr. Keenan also told me I was probably one of the smartest people who will testify in this case, and I was doing exactly what I should be doing up there. However, he did request that I stop giving Leroy death stares because it doesn't look good to the jury.

Later people would say that that fire drill was sent by Michelle to give me a chance to gather my thoughts. I guess they were right because it was a break I needed very much.

The next few hours the defense attorney would try his best to prove his case, but not by trying to prove Leroy innocent, instead he was going to try to create "reasonable doubt" in the minds of the jurors by shifting the blame towards me. The theory which he would try to prove was based solely on the idea that "I" was somehow able to leave my pick up route at FedEx around five p.m. or so, and travel ten miles back to Michelle's and my townhouse, (about twenty plus minutes at that time of day), kill Michelle then leave to go back to my route sometime before six p.m. and finish my job as if nothing happened. However, all the while I was scanning packages every three to five minutes or so with my tracker, and transmitting my data and exact whereabouts to dispatch via our on board computer. His theory on this was that I picked up thirteen of my stops early and scanned the packages into the tracker later thereby, as he stated, "fudged" my records to create an alibi.

FedEx trackers are equipped with a clock that cannot be changed by the user. Instead the tracker is plugged into a transmitter at the station, which is connected to a hub computer in Memphis, Tennessee. Any information that has been scanned into the tracker can then be transmitted to the central computer, and likewise any programming information the tracker needs, i.e. zip codes, time and date, is sent back to the tracker. So, it was established early on that it was not possible for me or anyone else to change the time registered in my tracker.

I was given a copy of the computerized pick up log for the day of the murder, and the defense attorney went through it with me minute by minute stop by stop looking for any minutes of spare time he could find that would have allotted me enough time to take off the hour between five and six p.m. Now I don't care how good someone is at their job it would be pretty nerve racking for an attorney to pull a day at random out of working past and analyze it for errors in front of a jury. My regular day consisted of forty to fifty stops collecting seventy-five to one hundred packages and letters. I was averaging thirteen stops an hour with the hours between four and six p.m. being my heaviest time.

Some of my stops were regular and I would go to them everyday, but more then half of them were customer call in stops which could be anywhere in my forty-two square mile route. Each of my stops was assigned a number based on the time that the call would come in. As I would make a pick up at a stop I had to punch the stop assigned number into the tracker, and scan the packages into the system that I got at that stop. When I got back to the truck I would plug the tracker into the on board computer, and all the data from the tracker would be transmitted into the worldwide system computer. That data would include the stop number and package air bill numbers. After the transmission was complete the stop number is taken off my list of stops and the dispatcher would know where I was and at what time.

This was all a very complicated way of trying to say that is was impossible for me or any courier at FedEx to manipulate the time package or stop. Not to mention the extreme volume of stops and packages we were faced with in such a short time.

Apparently, no one had expressed this fact to the defense attorney who was going through the whole record line by line to find any inconsistencies. He questioned the order in which I made my stops, and asking me if I recall the number of packages at any given stop. After a couple of hours of this I was getting to the end of my patience. When all of a sudden he found something. It seems that at one of my stops around 6PM my tracking log showed I scanned in three packages, but the defense attorney had a copy of the hand written shipping log the customer had all couriers sign when they picked up packages. The customer's log had a place for the drivers to write the shipping company name, the driver signed there name, and write the number of packages picked up there. I looked at it for a moment and saw where I had wrote Federal Express under company then there was my signature.... but under number of packages I had written four. My pick up log said three but I wrote in four. The defense attorney had a look on his face like he just produced the murder weapon with my fingerprints on it. What made it even worse, was that earlier I testified that I called Michelle at home that night to get a busy signal from that very location.

The defense attorney asked me. "Mr. Forte can you tell me why your records show three packages and you wrote in four on the customer's log?" He had a grin on his face that said *I gotcha kid.*

"Objection," Mr. Keenan said jumping up, "your honor the prosecution has not seen this new evidence that the defense is presenting. I would like a recess for a chance to review this new evidence."

The judge agreed to a recess, but the defense attorney wanted to approach the bench to argue. So, the prosecutor, defense attorney and the judge talked for a minute at the bench so the jury and spectators could not hear, but I could hear everything.

There was an argument between the two attorneys. The prosecutor said that he needed to be presented with this evidence before trial. But the defense argued that this information was as much available to the prosecution as it was to the defense. All he had to do was go get it from the company he got it from. Well thankfully the judge agreed with the prosecution and called a recess until the next morning to give Mr. Keenan an opportunity to review the new evidence.

As we were leaving the court room Mr. Keenan looked upset and asked my father and I to come with him to his office. My dad had been a Federal Express courier for twenty years at the time and Mr. Keenan was very interested in his expertise on the matter.

First my dad asked to see the copy of the log that I was looking at on the stand. He looked at if for a few seconds and sure enough he only saw three package air bill numbers for that stop. Then he asked if Mr. Keenan had the original printout of the document because he felt something was not right about this copy. Mr. Keenan did have the original printout with him and took it out. Dad looked at it a few seconds, and there it was the fourth package. You see, these reports were printed on the letter sized data paper that is connected together, and sometimes information can print on the perforated lines that are used to separate the sheets of paper. The original document had not been torn to separate the pages so you could read the air bill number of that fourth package perfectly right across the top of the page, but it was too close to the top of the page to have been picked up by the copy machine.

So there you have it. In less then five minutes my dad had solved the mystery, and shot down the defenses argument. We were all very relieved, especially Mr. Keenan who by this time had a huge smile on his face, and I looked forward to explaining this to the defense attorney back in court the next day.

The great thing was that all I could think about all night was how good it was going to feel to shoot down that attorney's argument. But what was even better was I knew he was probably so excited by the fact that he was finally going to be able to corner me with this. Only one of us could be right.

☞

The next morning I took the stand to finish my questioning by the defense. He reiterated the facts he had first posed the day before. He emphasized his point that my shipping record showed three packages and the log I signed showed four.

He swaggered up to me just radiating confidence, and said, "Can you explain this difference in your records?"

I answered, "Yes, I can."

I could tell this was not the answer he expected by a long shot, but after a second he went with it. "You can? Then how do you explain it?"

"Well", I said, "I did pick up four packages. Mr. Keenan has the original printout of the report, which shows the fourth package is really at the very top of the page and not visible on this copy you gave me. It looks like there was an error in the copying process."

At that point Mr. Keenan stood up with the top page of the original printout in his hand, and each page was still connected together linking down to a stack of paper on the table. The defense attorney looked like he had his pants pulled down in the girl's locker room. He was in shock, but that quickly turned to anger when he walked over to look at the original document.

Then he said with a tone of obvious frustration in his voice." Your honor, let the record show I was given inadequate information by the prosecution."

Well if the questions he asked before were grabbing at straws, the next couple hours of questioning were definitely out there. I'm fairly sure he was making up this line of questioning on the spot. I was asked; why didn't you buy your lunch everyday instead of coming home? Couldn't you take two or three dollars out of the ATM for lunch? When you called Michelle and got a busy signal why didn't you drop everything and rush home? Can you tell me why your pubic hairs were found in your bedroom? Why was a pair of your underwear found on the floor in your bedroom?

However, I really started to get very close to loosing my temper with him when he began accusing me of hitting Michelle. I hadn't hit anyone since the fifth grade, but this guy was getting real close when he tried to say I was a wife beater. He said there were neighbors, whose names he could not mention, who witnessed me slapping Michelle in the face in the townhouse parking lot. He also said Michelle's friends, who he also could not name, told him Michelle was afraid of me because I would hit her and slap her around. He could not produce one of these so-called witnesses he talked about. He was really getting close to setting me off, but I had to remain calm because if I got angry with him I would just prove his point that I had a violent temper. Up until now I took most of his questioning with a grain of salt, but now he was accusing me of doing something that boiled my blood. The idea that I could ever raise my hand to Michelle was not something I would even consider, and here he was trying to defend his client, a murderer, by trying to make me out as a wife beater. I could hardly sit in my seat while he badgered me over and over again about what a horrible husband I was for hitting my wife.

When the defense attorney finally concluded his questions, Mr. Keenan stood up to ask me some final questions to get the focus back on the murder.

"Joe," he said, "if somehow you had known that when you called Michelle and got a busy signal, that she actually had been murdered or was in a struggle for her life, would you have rushed home?"

Tears started to well up in my eyes, "Yes", I said meekly.

"Did you love Michelle, Joe?"

"Yes I did." Tears were now streaming down my face.

"No further questions Joe, you can come down."

I did manage to come across fairly well and contain my anger through that part of my testimony, but it really took everything I had emotionally to do it. In the end his whole line of questioning toward me, over seven hours spanning two days, was solely to get the focus off Leroy as a suspect and on to me. He never asked me one question about Leroy, and I don't even think he used his name or referred to him once during my questioning.

In the end I was glad to be done with it all, and I felt I did the best I could for Michelle. The defense walked away with nothing positive to help his case, and all I hoped for was that the jury and everyone watching was able to see how very much I loved her.

CHAPTER 18

The trial would go on for a total of three weeks. The remaining witnesses were police officers and detectives, forensic experts, and maintenance guys from around the complex. Since there was no chance I would be called again Mr. Keenan thought after the first week it might be best that I go back to Atlanta because there was nothing I could really do there. So, I stayed in Rochester for the rest of that week watching the trial on television each day to see what was going on.

I learned a lot about the actual case they had against Leroy that week. Even though I knew what the police and the prosecutor were focused on with regard to my part as a witness, I did not know how they had it all pieced together. Leroy would never testify on his own behalf, so we may never know exactly what took place, but the evidence drew a pretty good road map as to what had happened.

As Michelle and I had both figured, Leroy's live in girlfriend Karen, moved out of their townhouse the Sunday prior to Michelle's murder. There was some sort of argument going on that led Karen to call the police who helped her get her things safely out of the townhouse. We never heard from her again. Leroy was probably extremely angry over the break-up, and he wanted to focus that anger he had for Karen on someone else.

Three days after Karen left, on the day Michelle was murdered, Leroy met with his parole officer that afternoon. Leroy was on parole after serving two years of a four-year sentence for assaulting an elderly women and stealing her purse. His parole officer would later confirm the visit and said Leroy seemed just fine, and that he had no reason to expect anything was wrong with him that day.

In the meantime Michelle had left the house to do a little shopping at the mall. I'm not really sure what it was she bought, but the police had receipt copies and witnesses that would show she had been at the mall somewhere around five p.m. When she was done she headed back home to get ready for play practice that night. She was probably home by five thirty p.m. Michelle then took a shower.

The shower or running water could be heard from both our townhouse and Leroy's. It had been obvious to us when Karen or Leroy would take a shower because we could hear the water. This was when Leroy took his chance at getting into our townhouse. He had our key, which he previously made a copy of, so he let himself in. First he went to the kitchen where he took a knife out of our counter-top knife holder and cut the cord to the kitchen phone receiver. He threw the receiver onto the living room couch and walked upstairs to our bedroom. Seeing our bedroom phone he cut the cord on that receiver which left no working phones in the townhouse. Leroy then hid himself probably behind the closet door in our bedroom.

Michelle had left the television on to catch the news or maybe for a little company as we often did. When she was finished showering she came back into our room where she dried off. That was when he attacked her from behind. Leroy grabbed her with his left arm around her body, and with his right he slit her throat very deeply from ear to ear. Michelle then reached up to grab her throat and fell face down on the floor.

That first wound was enough to kill her, but she was probably alive for a few more agonizing moments as Leroy would stab her another ten times in the back. Some of the stab wounds were so fierce the knife went through Michelle and got lodged in the floor where he would have to wiggle the knife back and forth to force it out only to strike again and again. (When the investigators pulled up the carpet in the area where Michelle's body was laying, they could see the knife marks in the wood floor.)

When he was through he took the pair of panties Michelle was wearing before her shower and cut them at the seam. He then took the panties and my purple bathrobe, which was now splattered with blood and brought them down to our basement. Going to the kitchen he washed off the knife and put it back in the knife holder. Leroy then took the keys to Michelle's Volvo and left our townhouse for his. On the way out he left some blood on the wall beside the front door, and he did not lock or close the front door all the way.

Back at his townhouse he tried to quickly clean up his cloths putting his shirt in the washing machine and using almost a whole box of soap. He then left in Michelle's car and went to see some friends to borrow some money to get out of town. After milling around town for a while he returned to our neighborhood where he saw the swarm of police cars parked outside of our duplex. So, he continued driving past the parking lot and left the car on a residential street about a half-mile away. He then walked through the yards and back to our duplex where he ran into one of our neighbors. Leroy asked her what was going on, and she said the young girl who lived in our townhouse had been stabbed to death. Then he said, "Oh no.... not Michelle."

That was when he walked up to Patty's place and let himself in. That was the moment I saw him and we embraced.

When the investigators testified, the story he told them on the day he was arrested was quite a bit different. He did admit to seeing Michelle moments before she was murdered, and he also admitted to seeing her moments after she was murdered, however, the ten to fifteen minute interval between those two meetings he said he was not there.

Leroy would explain to the police that on the day Michelle was killed he went over to our townhouse around five thirty p.m. to use our phone. He said his phone had not been connected yet and needed to make a phone call. (One of our complex's maintenance men testified that he did some work at Leroy's townhouse earlier that afternoon, and that he was able to use the phone at Leroy's that day.) This would also be a good way to explain how his fingerprints were found on our phone.

After Leroy used our phone, he said Michelle let him take her car to go to Wegman's a local grocery store about one mile from our townhouse to purchase grape flavored Kool Aid and sugar. During the investigation Wegman's pulled their computerized sales journals to find that no one purchased grape Kool aid and sugar within a four hour period surrounding the murder.

When Leroy got back to our townhouse to return Michelle's car he said he found the front door open, so he walked upstairs to see if Michelle was okay. That was the moment he said he found Michelle's body covered in blood on the floor of our bedroom. In a panic he said he picked her up to see if there was anything he could do, but when he realized she was dead he decided he had better leave town for fear the police would suspect him because of his status as a convict on parole. This was his attempt to explain the blood found on him and the reason his fingerprints were found in the car.

The coroner would refute Leroy's statement that he picked Michelle up minutes after she was killed because when Michelle's body was being removed she had stiffened and her hands had to be prided from around her own neck. They believe when her throat was first cut she reached up to grab her throat where they remained after she dropped to the floor. If Leroy picked her up when he said he did Michelle's hands would have fallen away from her neck.

Leroy would later brag to an investigator in the police station, "Look, I know all about finger prints and blood testing. You may be able to arrest me, but you'll never convict me."

CHAPTER 19

I was pretty much a prisoner in my own parent's house since the hype was at its highest point in a year. This was the first local trial broadcast on TV in Rochester and if you didn't catch it live the nightly news and newspaper filled you in on most of the details everyday. Leroy's, Michelle's and my pictures were all over the city, and according to most everyone I knew people were saying it was the topic of the day everywhere in town.

I tried very hard to separate myself from it all, but sometimes it just takes a little thing to set you off and remind me that this was no movie... it was my life now. One evening that week my family, about fifteen of us in all, met at an Italian restaurant for dinner. It was a way everyone could show support for me when I needed them. Before I got there my father was waiting at the bar for a table and everyone else to get there.

While he was standing there he overheard a conversation a female bartender was having with two male customers. The topic was the trial. The men were saying they had been following it and they believed Leroy was guilty, and that the prosecution was building a strong case against him.

The bartender on the other hand had another opinion. " I think you're wrong, the husband was the one who did it, and they are just trying to pin it on the black guy."

My dad was shocked, but he kept his composure. He said he was worried that anything he said could reflect negatively on me. So, he calmly reached in his wallet and pulled out one of his business cards from Federal Express, and laid it on the bar then he walked away. If the bartender was following the trial like she said she was that was a subtle clue to her that you never know who is listening to you.

When I got there and after the family was seated I looked over at my dad and I could see he was pretty upset. When I asked him what was wrong he did not want to tell me, but after I badgered him for a while he told me what had just taken place up at the bar. Right there, in a crowded restaurant.... I lost it. I hadn't cried like that since my Aunt Natalie's wedding five months earlier. It hurt me deeper then I ever thought it could. I couldn't believe I was so effected by what a stranger had to say about my guilt or innocence.

When you are innocent you would do anything to prove to every last person in the world that you are innocent. But, if you are guilty the only opinion you care about is the opinion expressed by the twelve jurors whose job it is to judge you. As I sat there and cried, with my family all around me in a very public place, any doubt that I had about leaving town before the trial ended quickly left my mind.

So, after being in Rochester for about ten days I left to go back to Atlanta. Now my body was there, but my mind was not. I talked to my family everyday to get an update on the trial.

Back at work the cat was out of the bag about why I was gone for more then a week. Before I left for the trial I explained what was going on to my manager, who when I transferred to Atlanta was told by co-workers in Rochester only that my wife had died and that they wanted her to "take care of me". She had no real idea of the magnitude of what had truly happened until I told her.

Even though my official absence was classified as jury duty everyone I worked with knew where I was really going and why. At this point I was glad everyone knew because with all that had gone on I really needed to talk about it with people who cared about me, and there were no shortage of ears to listen. These people had now known me for close to a year and the kind of person I was, so it now felt right for them to know about my past. I even made copies of articles from the Rochester paper about the trial so they could all have a good understanding. All of them were so good to me and they helped support me during that time.

Within a few days the defense wrapped up his case, and to my recollection I don't think he called any of his witnesses. Not even those he claimed told him I was a wife beater, because they did not exist. The jury deliberated for more then fifteen hours over two days. They asked to see some of the evidence and hear some of the transcribed witness testimony.

They took their job very seriously and did not rush to reach a verdict. Even though these were the longest two days of my life when it was over I was very glad they had taken their time to be sure. In my mind at least this was an answer to those who believed this "all white jury" could not judge this case fairly.

The one day I wished I was back up there was the day the jury read their verdict. "Guilty of second degree murder." My family called me immediately from the courthouse to tell me the news. I was so relieved. I felt like a huge weight had been lifted off of me, and at that moment I felt back on top of the world for the first time in a very long time.

Once the verdict was in I was able to concentrate on finishing out the school term, which was about a month away from ending. I was told the sentencing would take place some time in at the end of March. The timing worked out well for me because I wanted to fly back for the sentencing and it was an added relief to not have schoolwork waiting for me upon my return.

When I did go back to Rochester the media still had a very big interest in the story, but the original drama that was apparent when the murder first took place and through the trial had disappeared. This was the final chapter and all that was left was to show how those of us involved would handle the end and move on with the rest of our lives.

Once again I granted Wendy Wright from our local NBC station the only interview I was going to give. This time she met me at my parent's house the day before the sentencing for a one on one interview that was not going to be live this time.

I felt the questions were fair and centered on my feelings after the trial was finally over. I was also asked questions regarding how this whole ordeal had affected my life. I made the statement that I felt this past year had made me a stronger person and aside from this ever happening to me again I felt I was better prepared to handle adversity in my life.

She had also asked me how I felt about Leroy's comments that race had everything to do with the fact that he had been convicted.

My reply was that I felt race played absolutely no part in the case at all, and I also felt that the ninety-nine point ninety-nine percent of hard working honest African American citizens in Rochester should be angry that Leroy had leaned on his race like a crutch to describe the situation he put himself in. Race had nothing to do with anything as far as I was concerned, I would be just as determined to see justice done if the murderer had been white.

When the interview was done and the camera and microphone had been shut off Wendy had asked me if I would have preferred that Leroy would be given the death penalty, which was not an option in New York State at the time. I basically told her I would flip the switch myself if they would let me.

Now I did not know it at the time but when the interview aired later that evening on the six o'clock news I found out they had interviewed Leroy sometime during that day as well, and both our interviews were intermixed. First I would make a comment, then they would switch to Leroy for his response to the same question. As expected he adamantly denied murdering Michelle, and once again focused on race as the reason he was in jail in the first place. He said from the first moment he was sitting at the defense table and the "sea of white jurors" filed into the courtroom he knew he did not have a chance.

Even though the race issue was not an issue to me, the police, the prosecution or my family it was out there, and it was something I was being asked to answer too. Leroy's defense tried to make me out to be a murderer and a wife beater, and for the past year Leroy was trying to make the whole Monroe County Justice system and myself out to be racists to gain sympathy. The good thing was that the media was not buying into it, and Leroy was the only one making public statements about it. After hearing it from him for the past year it had lost it's meaning to me, and I was no longer going to let it effect me.

A local African-American leader the Rev. Raymond L. Graves of United Church Ministry, Inc. captured some print in the local paper with his harsh criticism of the prosecution and the jury system. The Reverend referred to the trial as a "kangaroo court", which I personally assume, means that it jumped to conclusions and judgment, at least in his eyes. He was quoted as saying " On Saturday an all-white jury convicted Leroy Anderson on circumstantial or no evidence just as all-white juries have done to black people ever since the jury system was established in America." He was even so bold to say on another occasion that, "They (the jury) worked hard, but it wasn't fair because he was convicted." He said he believed Leroy was innocent. *(The Reverend's quotes extracted from articles printed in the Rochester Democrat & Chronicle and Times Union)*

At this point I expected as much from self appointed community leaders like Graves, so I tried not to let comments like that bother me anymore either, because I knew even among the people he claimed to represent his comments were in the minority. Since the trial was covered word for word on local television I felt even better about it because nothing was hidden. I also was not going to let the opinions of others anger me anymore. As far as the New York State criminal justice system was concerned, justice was done and done fairly.

The day of sentencing felt a lot different than the trial did for me. Gone now was the uncertainty of the trial's outcome, and the pressure for me to testify. Mr. Keenan had assured me the judge would probably sentence Leroy to the maximum sentence the state allows of twenty-five years to life for second-degree murder, (first degree murder being reserved for police officers and public officials.) That sentence however, left the door open for possible parole, but not until he has served his minimum of twenty-five years. Leroy was led into the courtroom escorted by the two guards who were with him at trial.

As victims, my mother-in-law Catina and myself were given the opportunity to give what is called a victims impact statement before sentencing is handed down. That would give us the chance to let the court, and Leroy know, how his actions have affected our lives. Strangely enough, I was looking forward to this, and I don't remember feeling the least bit nervous about it. However, no matter what I said I wasn't going to truly be able to describe to Leroy what it had been like, to be me this past year, but I was going to try.

Before it was our chance to speak, to start off the sentencing hearing Mr. Keenan described Michelle as a person, and what her loss meant to those who knew her and the Rochester community as a whole. Mr. Keenan also described the absolute brutality and senselessness of Michelle's murder by Leroy Anderson.

Mr. Keenan then gave a brief history of Leroy's past experiences with the criminal justice system. Leroy's past crimes were not admissible in court during the trial, so for me, this was the first time that I was going to hear some of the horrible crimes he had been convicted of in the past.

There were three incidents where Leroy had attacked women and assaulted them. Twice before he had attacked women from behind and beaten them severely. The first offense took place when he was a teenager and for that he was sentenced as a youthful offender. For his second offense he was sentenced to probation, and it was during that probation period that he brutally attacked a sixty-one year old woman and took her purse. For that offense he was sentenced to four years in prison, of which he served two years, and he was on parole from that sentence at the time he murdered Michelle.

This made me think that our system of criminal justice and punishment was an absolute joke. How could a person keep committing the same type of crime over and over again, and each time more severe than the last, but just keep getting away with it. If he had been in prison where he belonged, Michelle still would have been here.

After Mr. Keenan finished it was our turn. First up to give her statement was Catina. Her speech was a wonderful tribute to Michelle's talent for music, and her infectious enthusiasm for life. She also spoke of her own inability to enjoy the sweetness of life after what Leroy had done to her daughter. She closed saying, that Michelle would never get to hold her own child in her arms as she once held Michelle.

Catina's words were beautiful, and I must admit they made me think about exactly what she had lost with the death of her own child. I stopped feeling bad for myself, and tried to think of exactly what she was going through. Realistically I knew I never could.

I was next and called to step forward. I walked through the visitors' seating area passed Leroy and both attorneys. I stood at a podium and my back was to everyone except the judge. Although I do not remember the speech I gave word for word it went something like this...

Michelle wasn't the only one who died that night, but a piece of everyone who knew her died too. Especially me, my world revolved around her. Never again will I see her smiling face, or hear her laugh, or hear her say, "I Love you Joey."

Michelle will also never be able to be a mother to her own children. I know she would have been the best mother any child could ever have. (At that point I was struggling to hold back tears).

Mr. Anderson however, by his actions that night took that all away from her, and those of us who loved her. So, I would ask this court to give him the maximum sentence allowed by law, twenty-five years to life, and never to allow him to get out of prison. Anything less then that would be a miscarriage of justice.

When I turned around to walk back to my seat there was not a dry eye from anyone except Leroy's family. Leroy gave me the same cold-hearted stare he did at the trial, but this time I did not return the favor. Mr. Keenan looked at me and slowly nodded his head in approval. I knew then I had done all I could do to help bring justice, and I felt peace.

The last person to speak before the sentence was handed down was Leroy. All during the trial he had not spoken a word on his own behalf. So, I truly expected a sorrowful plea for mercy, but what he came out with was the total opposite. His statement was loaded with expletives, and the use of the "F word" as a verb and an adjective.

He started by saying he grew up in a rough neighborhood, where he had to "do the deeds to earn his stripes". He said, "This trial was racial from day one. How could I have been found not guilty by an all white jury? If the woman was black I might've had a shot."

"There is so much anger inside of me," he said " I don't feel sympathetic for nothing." He expressed anger toward Michelle's mother and I for requesting he be given life in prison.

"The simple fact is I did not do this. I wish to God you would have took he out back and hung me from a tree. I'm not asking for leniency because all through the trial you ain't done nothing but f**k me, keep f**king me. Give me twenty-five years. That is what I'm asking for."

*(Leroy's Quotes were extracted from the Rochester Democrat &
Chronicle and Times Union Newspapers)*

After that speech most people thought I would have been mad,
but it was the total opposite. I could not contain my joy at the dis-
play he had just put on. He had finally shown his true colors, and
any chance he had of gaining any sympathy from anyone was gone.
During his speech I was struggling to hold back a smile, and at
times outright laughter. The whole trial he had been so stoic. He
tried to portray himself as the innocent victim. He would have been
better off keeping quiet. Frankly, I though this was a far better
response than remorse from him.

Then Judge Mark said a few words before handing down the sentence. He mentioned he had received over two hundred letters from
family; friends and even concerned members of the community asking him to hand down the toughest sentence allowable. The Judge
then said, that for reasons known only to him and God he took a
beautiful and wonderful person's life. So, he handed him the
twenty-five year sentence we had all asked for. He also noted he
would write a letter recommending Leroy never get out of prison,
ever.

With that, Leroy was taken away, and I have never seen him in
person since. The long ordeal was over and now I hoped to find
some peace.

As we left the courtroom, the press surrounded us. They had cameras and microphones and were pushing them in our faces. Catina
and I led everyone to the D.A.'s meeting room where we agreed to
give a statement.

I was asked about my reaction to Leroy's statements inside the
courtroom, and I answered, that "Leroy is a very bitter man with a
lot of anger, but he has no one to blame but himself for his situation." I continued, " I am glad the trial is now behind us and now I
feel I can now start mourning the loss of my wife."

Catina and I hugged while camera bulbs were flashing all around
us. I did not know it then, but that would also be the last time I
would see her as well.

After the press conference I wanted to catch the defense attorney
because I had a few choice words for him. As I came up behind him

I called out his name. Quickly, he turned around, and he appeared a bit nervous to talk with me face to face outside the courtroom. He offered me his hand to shake, and after looking at it for what was an awkward five seconds for him, I offered mine in return.

"Joe, I'm sorry for your loss," he said. "I hope you don't take anything I said in there personal I was just doing my job. If you were in Leroy's position you would have wanted someone like me to defend you."

I looked at him with a smug smirk as I slowly shook my head from side to side. Then I put my hand on his shoulder and said, "I don't think so." Then I just walked away feeling totally satisfied that I had gotten my point across without saying more then four words.

Back in the D.A.'s office there was champagne and a lot of congratulations for everyone. Sgt. Mulkin was there, and I thanked him for all his hard work and that of the Greece police department. He was glad that things had turned out the way they did.

I asked him if he had really thought the day he was questioning me if I was really capable of doing such a thing. He answered, "I wasn't sure, but we had to do what we did." The Sergeant also later mentioned to me about some things one of Michelle's friends had told him about the night of the break-in on December 17th. Apparently among the underwear that had been thrown around our room, Michelle had found a pair that had semen on it. She never told me, but instead just threw it away because she did not want me to get upset.

That is one of the things that led investigators to believe Leroy may have stalked Michelle for some sexual fantasy. I never knew that, and it wasn't even brought out in trial. I had an uneasy feeling though that if only I had really known what he was up to I could have stopped Michelle from ever being murdered.

CHAPTER 20

The day after the sentencing was over my parents flew back with me to Atlanta to stay for a visit over the Easter holiday, which was the following weekend. We had picked up a local newspaper at the airport, which had a huge picture of Leroy on the front page taken during his speech at sentencing.

As we sat in the plane waiting for take-off I was of course reading the article, which followed the picture. I did not know if there was anyone on the plane who had recognized me, but after all I had been through over the past couple of months I did not care either way. I was really happier then I had been in a very long time, and I now felt closure of this chapter, and I was eager to start living my life again.

Once we arrived back in Atlanta it was like when I first had moved there, I was filled with excitement to be back and I was ready to get back to school. After a couple of months though, just like the year before, the good feeling had started to go away. I was feeling lonely and missed Michelle. I thought maybe if I started dating again, and enjoying the company of a woman that I would find what I thought I was missing.

I was relying more and more on my tarot cards and advice from spiritual advisors. Praying to God and reading the Bible were also part of my search for guidance. I would even go so far as placing my Bible and rosary around the Tarot cards as I was reading them, to hopefully elicit help from God. I would do the cards over and over again until I got favorable answers to the questions I was seeking. Mainly I wanted to know if the woman I was going to love was out there, and when was I going to meet her. I also wanted to know what was I going to do after school was over, where was I to go. As Leroy was filing his appeals I wanted to know the outcomes, and if he was going to somehow get a new trial.

I would have tarot card reading sessions that went on for hours as I sat in a dark room with only ritualistic candles all around to allow me to read the Bible and my how-to tarot card book. I was really mixing God with New Age and frankly neither was giving me the hope and support I was looking for. However that did not stop me from coming back, night after night, to consult those cards. To see if God was listening to me I would ask Him to move the cross on my rosary as it lay in the palm of my hand, but He never did.

I thought that after the trial all this would no longer affect me but I was wrong. I still had very disturbing fantasies about killing Leroy. Before the trial many of my plans were set along the line of, "How would I go about killing him if he got out?" I ran through these plans over and over again until I thought they were perfect. I felt if I had done it I could have easily gotten away with it because chances are no one would care enough about him to bother to look for me.

These fantasies however were now replaced with the scenarios of how I was going to get on the inside of the prison to kill him. I dreamed of becoming an inmate in his prison where the only goal in my mind was to kill Leroy. I had it all figured out, and I did not even care if I spent my life in prison I just wanted him dead. I had so much anger still inside me, and the more I thought about that weak sentence the angrier I got. Death was the only thing I felt was a good enough punishment for him.

Here he was in prison. He did not have to work, pay bills or fight traffic everyday. He had it too good.

Mostly I worked hard to repress those feelings of anger or else I could not make it through each day. I did, however, allow myself time to let those feelings come out, always alone, at night, and usually after drinking heavily. The problem was when I would let all these feelings come out they never seemed to all fit back in the box neatly again, and I would feel their lingering effects for a few days. After those few days were over I would feel better until the next wave would hit me usually in a month or two.

At this point I felt the answer to stabilizing this up and down emotional wave was to start dating again. I did not just wake up one day and decide, "Okay, today I start dating." it was more like an evolutionary decision. Over the past year while hanging out with Rick and his wife Michelle, we had a large circle of friends which included women who I developed very good platonic friendships with like Jen and Melissa, who were college friends of theirs.

All of my life I have felt more comfortable sharing my emotions like pain or sadness with women. So, now I really wanted to take my place outside of the comfortable group of friends, and start to develop my own relationships. Although, Rick and everyone had been a great source of strength to me, for my own healing I needed to move on. In June I had decided it was time I got my own apartment, and that was a good decision for all three of us. First, Rick and Michelle needed to spend time together in their own place alone as husband and wife, and secondly I needed to learn to live again by myself without fear.

I dated two different women that spring and early summer, but neither of these short relationships worked out very well. From the beginning of these brief relationships, I was open about what I had just gone through with Michelle's murder. I had made it very clear to them I did not know where I was heading emotionally, and that I was not going to commit or promise myself to a woman at this point in my life. I told them I still had a lot of healing left to do, and all I was looking for was their companionship.

The first woman and I just slowly drifted apart because what each of us wanted wasn't what we were going to get from the other. The second woman however, in spite of what I would keep telling her as to where I stood in our relationship, she still would try to cling to me tighter. The more I would pull away the tighter she would cling. I was not ready for something like this at all. I was not in a place in my life where I had the ability to fulfill someone else's emotional needs, so I had to break it off.

Rick saw the difficulty I was having in those few short months, and he thought there was a young woman at his company who might be a good match for me. I told him I would be interested in calling her, so acting as my middleman Rick approached her on my behalf. After looking at a picture on Rick's desk of Todd, Rick and myself at his wedding she agreed to give him her number so I could call her. That young woman, Rachel Richards, would change my life.

CHAPTER 21

The first time I called Rachel was a weeknight, and we spoke for over three hours. I immediately could tell from our conversation she was strong, intelligent and independent. We had agreed to meet the following Saturday to see a movie and have dinner. After the phone conversation I told Rick I did not care what she looked like because I knew right then I had made a life long friend.

On July 23rd, we had our first date. We met at the movie theater; both of us drove our own cars. Rachel told me what model car she would be driving so I knew how to find her. When I saw her walking through the parking lot I was stunned by how beautiful she was. She had insisted on paying for the movie herself. We saw *Forest Gump*, with Tom Hanks, and I remember thinking through the whole thing how wonderful she smelled, all I wanted to do was hold her hand, but I didn't.

After the movie we went to get something to eat, and then back to her apartment to watch videos. We talked all night. She was so great I could not believe it because this was the first time since Michelle I had felt so emotionally close to another woman. I remember how nervous I was before our first kiss. I wanted nothing more then to just feel her lips on mine. When I finally did kiss her at the end of the evening I felt chills the moment our lips touched, and right then I had a strong feeling the two of us had chemistry together.

We made arrangements to see each other the next day, and that was when I told her about what had happened to Michelle. It did not seem to bother her or intimidate her one bit. Rachel had lost a boyfriend in a motorcycle accident four years earlier, and her mother died in a car accident when she was only six years old. So, there was a special bond between us since each of us had experienced the loss of someone we loved at a similar period in our lives.

Although it was never formally spoken, from that time forward Rachel and I were exclusively together. Almost everyday we talked on the phone, and saw each other two to three times a week.

On August 1st, Rachel along with Rick and Michelle helped me move into my new apartment. The new place was only about two miles from where I lived with Rick, but now I was really on my own.

As our relationship progressed through the rest of that summer and into fall, I was keeping up my hectic schedule at school and work, finishing two quarter-terms in that period of time. Rachel and I continued our relationship, but I had made it known to her that finishing school was my main priority. I felt if she wanted to stay, that was great, but if not that was fine too. I had a goal and I did not want to lose my focus.

Rachel was very patient with me. She never tried to pressure me into a deeper commitment than I was willing to give, and gave me space and time alone when I asked for it without trying to make me feel guilty about it. We never took any breaks from our relationship, but there were times when I told her I needed to spend a few days by myself.

At Thanksgiving that year I made my first family trip with her to visit her mother's side of the family in Vicksburg, Mississippi. Now I had never been in that part of the country except to drive through once on our way to New Orleans. At first I was a bit nervous to meet her extended family, but once we arrived I felt a strong sense of belonging amongst all of them. My up bringing as a first generation Italian-American Catholic in the suburbs of Upstate New York was culturally a lot different from theirs in the Deep South. However, there was one thing that remained the same, and that was the strength and closeness of her family.

Rachel had already told her Aunt Linda, (her mother's sister) and her grandparents the basics about what had happened to Michelle. Her Aunt Linda later mentioned to Rachel that because of the tragedies their family had gone through there was already a common bond between them and myself. Not only was Rachel's mother killed in a car accident at twenty-four, but her mother's brother was also killed when he was around the same age in a motorcycle accident. Rachel's grandparents Albert and Margie had lost two of their five children before they even had a chance to live. Also when her Grandfather was a young man running the family dairy farm he lost his right arm in a farming accident that changed the lives and direction of the whole family.

This was a strong loving family who had endured too many hardships, and all through it they were able to keep their faith in God. Rachel's Grandfather is probably the most courageous and spiritual men I have ever known. Although we never discussed every detail of what each of us had gone through in our lives, he was very open with me and shared his faith and knowledge with me, which was more of an encouragement then he could have ever realized.

As Rachel and I were leaving to head back to Atlanta, her Grandmother gave us a book about relationships. She said she saw something in the two of us that gave her the feeling we were meant to be together. Rachel and I smiled at one another at the thought of it, but we never mentioned anything further about it. That visit had made a very strong impression on me, and it had made me see Rachel in a way I hadn't seen her before, interacting in a loving family.

Soon after we arrived home the Christmas season was beginning to get underway. I had finished what was to be my next to last college quarter right around Thanksgiving, and I was finally seeing the end of my goal in sight.

Rachel and I had attended a party at the home of one of my professors, who a few months earlier had taken the class on a field trip to the U.S. Federal Penitentiary in Atlanta. I was disappointed at the time at how clean it was, and I was also hoping to see the inmates suffering more. We were told however, that most of the prisoners we saw were mainly there on drug convictions. Most murderers were actually in state prisons and not in federal. That trip did have an effect on me, but it certainly wasn't to make me too sympathetic.

However, there was one man that I had met there that touched me in a way I didn't expect. As our class was walking from one building to another a group of prisoners were leaving their work detail and heading back to the main building. While in federal penitentiaries most non-violent prisoners have the opportunity to work jobs inside the prison. At the Atlanta facility prisoners produced and repaired U.S. Mail bags and military combat fatigues for the U.S. Army.

Anyway, as the group of prisoners was walking by us, an African-American man who must have been in his sixties with a long gray beard and bushy gray hair, looked at me and asked if myself, and the rest of my class, were studying to be lawyers. I just smiled at him and replied, "Yes, some of us are".

Then he said, "Good, maybe then you can help me get out of this place when you graduate." I could not believe how much compassion I was feeling for that man. I don't know if it was God speaking to my heart or what, but to me there was a man in front of me who at that very moment was in despair and without a future. He seemed sad, lonely and like all hope was gone. I could not help but feel sorry for him. I didn't ask him what he had done because I didn't want to know. As far as I was concerned this was just an ordinary man in front of me who made some bad choices in his life. I think I took some of that prison with me when I left that day.

Well, the party at my professor's house happened to take place around the time of what would have been Michelle's and my second wedding anniversary. When Rachel and I went back to my apartment after, we sat on my couch looking at my Christmas tree. To say the least my decorations were a far cry from those of Christmas past. I had a small, potted live tree that stood all of a foot tall, pot included, with a single strand of lights around my patio doors.

I told Rachel that Michelle's and my anniversary was soon approaching, and how hard this time of the year was for me. She placed my head on her shoulder and stroked my hair while I cried. I was so glad Rachel was there for me. I don't know what I would have done without her that night.

For the Christmas Holiday later that month I brought Rachel back home with me to Rochester. It was the first time I had been back since Leroy's sentencing, and I was really looking forward to this trip. I wanted to show Rachel around the place I grew up, and to have her meet my family. She had also not seen snow in quite a long time, so I hoped there would be a lot of it. Instead it was a very green Christmas that year, but no matter I was just happy to be back for a while.

My family as I expected, welcomed Rachel with open arms, and my mother especially tried very hard to make her feel at home. Like me, and the Thanksgiving trip Rachel and I took earlier, I could tell she fit right in with my family. To me this of course was no surprise, because that was probably why I was attracted to her in the first place.

At the end of the trip Rachel and I had once again made another "unspoken" advance in our relationship. However, this scared me more then I thought it would and I was about to put on the brakes and push her away. The last thing I wanted was to ever fall in love again, because then I would have to open myself up. I feared that once I started to care then I would have to face the possibility of losing someone I cared about again.

CHAPTER 22

The start of the New Year brought with it the start of my last quarter of college before graduation. I was so excited that my goal was finally within reach. The best thing about this quarter was that I wasn't going to spend much of it in class, but instead I was given an internship at the Georgia General Assembly, (the State of Georgia's legislative body).

The internship would give me enough credits for two classes, and I only needed one other class to graduate. My previously difficult schedule was about to get a bit tougher. The internship was full time eight a.m. until five p.m. everyday. Two nights a week I had class from seven p.m. until nine p.m., and the other three nights I worked at FedEx from six p.m. until ten p.m. and eight a.m. until five p.m. on Saturdays. This schedule left me very little time for Rachel. When I had free time I was either studying or sleeping.

Rachel was taking a night class at the university the same nights I was, so we would spend a little time together after class and on some Sundays studying. The amount of time we saw each other had gone down quite a bit, which was what I frankly wanted to happen. I felt if we didn't spend very much time together we might just drift apart. I wanted no part of any long term-committed relationship, and the thought of it scared me to death.

After a short time working at the State Capital I knew this is what I wanted to do with my life. I thought through government I could make a difference. The Georgia General Assembly met from January through March, forty legislative working days, so there wasn't much to do for the remaining nine months a year there. I had made up my mind that I was going to move to Washington, D.C. after graduation to pursue a career in politics.

I thought I could work for a Senator or Congressman, or maybe even a congressional committee as a staff person. While working with the State of Georgia I met a lot of influential people. I worked as a staff member for two different senators, and I spent a lot of time hanging around the Lt. Governor's office visiting with his staff members. I had gotten many compliments from the people I worked for and with, and everyone was willing to help me with recommendations and contacts when I moved to Washington.

I figured this was it. I found something I really enjoyed, and I felt I could really make a difference. I wanted so much to do something on a grand scale that would give my life a purpose. I wanted to fulfill my promise to Michelle and be able to help others, so this had to be the way I was going to do it. Love… I thought would just get in the way.

By about mid-February Rachel had been sensing for some time, that we were not as close as we had been just a few short months earlier. One Sunday afternoon she and I talked about where the two of us were heading together. For the first time in our relationship after dating over eight months without one word about it, Rachel brought up the subject of my commitment level. She also looked me in the eye, and told me, "You know now much I love you."

This was not what I wanted to hear and I replied, "I'm sorry but you are just not my priority right now, school and my future are." I truly felt bad saying that, the last thing I wanted was to hurt Rachel, but I could not tell her something I didn't feel, or was willing to allow myself to feel. I learned much later, that Rachel almost broke our relationship off that night, but she didn't. I know that I about broke her heart, but I couldn't allow myself to feel guilty about it. There was something she saw in me that I could not see for myself, so she stuck by me.

The end of March, 1995 brought graduation from college. My parents and my Aunt Natalie and Uncle Larry came to celebrate with me. Rachel threw me a surprise graduation party, and I couldn't remember feeling this good about myself in a very long time. I felt so proud and blessed to have such support from my family and friends. I worked hard and I accomplished my goal under very difficult emotional circumstances. I felt now I had prepared myself to make a difference in the world.

The next couple months were spent planning my move to Washington, D.C. Most of my planning however, involved the Tarot cards, or advise from my "spiritual advisors". This was my next big move and I did not get the revelation that I received when it was time to move to Atlanta. Instead this was just something that I thought I needed to do to move on with my political goals to make a difference in this world.

The whole time Rachel was right along side of me trying to support me as best she could. There were a few times when we were together that she was a bit quiet and distant, and other times she would broach the subject, ever so gently, of what my feelings were toward her. I also know that she saw that I myself might not have been totally convinced that moving to Washington was the best thing for me to do.

One Sunday afternoon Rachel brought me a book, *Embraced by the Light,* by Betty Eadie. It was a book about a woman who had a near death experience and saw and talked with Jesus during that time. Well after she had given me the book she began to talk with me about forgiveness.

"You know Joe," she said, "you will never be able to move on with your life and open your heart to love again unless you truly forgive Leroy for what he has done."

"Forgive Leroy?" I barked back, "You have got to be kidding me. I'm never going to forgive him ever."

"God says we can never be truly forgiven unless we forgive those who have done harm to us." She said this so calmly, but not in a preachy or judgmental way. Rachel was expressing genuine concern and relaying to me biblical truth.

"Look, I'm not forgiving Leroy, and I think God is just going to have to give me a pass on that one. He knows what Leroy has done to Michelle, and He will understand that I just can't forgive him ever."

She had to be kidding me. Please... forgive Leroy... I don't think so. My whole life was fueled on the hatred I held for him. He was my motivation for everything I was doing. I could not see that happening ever. I truly planned on going to my grave with contempt and hatred for him in my heart, and that was all there was to it. The conversation rang in my hears several times over the next few days and every time I thought about it my blood would begin to boil.

How could God ever expect me to forgive Leroy? If that is what God wanted of me, He could just forget it because it wasn't going to happen.

CHAPTER 23

On the second week of June of 1995 I was making my move to Washington. I had gotten a transfer once again with FedEx, but I had no intention of working there for very long. For a few months before leaving, I had been sending my resume to most of the conservative Georgia and New York Congressman and Senators with not one job offer. Once I got there however, I felt I would have an easier time.

About six weeks before the move I made my first visit to Washington and stayed with an old college friend Margaret, from my days at Kent State back in 1987, where I attended two years before transferring to SUNY Buffalo. I knew that city was where I wanted to be the first time I drove in on I-95 and caught my first ever sight of the Capitol Building in the morning sun.

I'll never forget standing on the bank of the Potomac River in front of the Jefferson Monument looking at the city lit up at night. My heart was so filled with emotion and pride that night, and I could not wait to be a part of that city. This is where I felt I needed to be to make a difference in the world.

Margaret re-introduced me to a friend of hers Dave, who was also from Kent State. We had met a few times before mostly at parties and gatherings Margaret had thrown over the years. He was currently staying at her place, but was looking for a place of his own. The two of us had decided it would be a good idea if we became roommates and got our own place together. So, I had left him to the task of finding us an apartment while I went back to Atlanta to get ready for the move. I sent him an eight hundred dollar deposit when he told me he found us a great apartment on the bottom floor of a house in Southeast Washington. I had seen a lot of those types of apartments when I made my visit so I was excited at the thought.

Rachel had taken a vacation from work to help me move up there. I was very grateful for her help, but I admit I was too excited to understand how she was feeling about me leaving. I rented a big twenty-four foot truck to make the trip, and I towed my car behind. I was leaving Atlanta the same way I came. Although I was looking forward to living in Washington, I could not help but feel sad leaving Atlanta. The city had been good to me, it helped me heal and grow when I needed to the most. It wasn't the same feeling of relief I had when I first left Rochester, it was more of an incomplete feeling. Like somehow there were still some things for me to accomplish there.

After Rachel and I had emptied out the apartment I went back in for a final look. I sat down on the living room floor and prayed to God hoping I was making the right decision. I was really going to miss that place and all the friends I had made in Atlanta, but I kept telling myself this is what I had to do. I sat on the floor of my apartment and just tried to take everything in for one last time.

I had experienced a lot of different emotions there from utter despair to glimpses of happiness. That apartment to me represented a big part of my healing process because it had been where I had gotten over the fear of staying alone. I was really going to miss it, but I thought it was time for me to move on.

If the ride up to Washington was any indication of what I was going to have in store for me, I should have turned around at the North Carolina/ South Carolina border and gone back to Georgia. The trip was just awful. The truck was so weighted down, and the gas pedal had governors, which would not allow it to go above fifty-five mph, and when we went up hills it barely reached forty-five mph. The steering wheel had a lot of play in it making it was a constant struggle for me to keep it on the road. When I made the trip by car six weeks earlier it took me nine hours, but this time it was over fifteen hours before we finally arrived in Washington.

We drove all night and all I wanted to do was go to my new apartment home when we got there. Although I was tired and a bit frustrated after the trip, the excitement of it all had me ready to go. We stopped at Margaret's first and Dave suggested Rachel and I get some rest. I insisted Rachel and I were fine and that we should just get going because I really wanted to get settled there. So Dave jumped in the front seat of the truck with Rachel and I and we headed off to my new home.

As we were driving he would tell me to take a left down a residential street and I would say, " Hey, this is pretty nice. Are we close?"

"No, not yet, a little further." Dave responded.

"Well is it like that street." I asked

"We couldn't afford to live on that street, but ours is pretty good" he answered.

After only a few miles the nice neighborhoods were starting to disappear, and we turned down a couple of meaner streets. I thought whoa, I hope I don't have to drive through this neighborhood to get home every night. Before you know it, Dave said, "Here is our street."

I could not believe it when I pulled up to this place. It was a mess, and in a very questionable neighborhood to say the least. There was garbage on the ground all over the front yard, and the front stairs to the place were broken. Bars were on all the windows, and it looked like the homeless had been using the front entranceway as shelter. The inside had a cold and dark feeling. In the kitchen half the cupboard doors were falling off and the stove and range hood were totally rusted. The previous tenant had left some rancid food in the refrigerator that was all stuck to the shelves.

I could not believe what I was seeing. There was no way I could live here. Not just because of the condition, but I felt an immediate uneasiness about it and I was sick to my stomach. The neighborhood scared me senseless. I still had quite a bit of anxiety from what had happened to Michelle, and to be honest I would have felt safer back in the apartment where she was killed. I was not happy at all. I would have never even considered this place if I was the one who was looking. Moving me in there would have been like moving someone who was claustrophobic into a coffin, my emotions just couldn't take it.

All David kept trying to do was sell me on the place. You would have thought the guy was getting a commission or something. "Isn't this great." he would say, "I love this neighborhood, it has such character with everyone hanging out on their front stairs."

"Yeah Dave, they are sitting out there selling drugs." I snapped.

"What is the matter with you dude, is this not what you expected." he started to sound patronizing, and that was getting me more upset. "I don't know what you thought we were going to get for eight hundred dollars a month in DC."

"Margaret pays half that and she lives in a great neighborhood." I snapped.

He leaned on the window sill and folded his arms and said in an accusing tone, "What is the matter Joe...do you have a problem with black people?"

I don't think he knew how close I was to pushing him out that window when those words came out of his mouth. "No." I answered after taking a deep breath, "I just don't feel safe in this neighborhood after all I have been though in my life, and there is no way I am going to live here. So, I don't care what you have to do to get our deposit back, but I am out of here."

After all the accusations of racism back in Rochester, I have to come to DC, where a white college boy from the suburbs like myself insinuates that I am a racist.

The whole way back to Margaret's we did not speak one word. When we got there Dave got on the phone to see if he could get our money back, and Rachel and I went for a walk. She was just as upset as I was, but she had a level head.

"Joe honey, don't worry." She said, "I will help you find a place, and I will even help loan you the money if you need it."

I was on the verge of tears; I did not know what to do. I felt like just leaving and going back to Atlanta. All I owned was in this truck and I had nowhere to live. There was no chance I would ever consider Dave as a roommate again, so I was going to have to do it alone. At this point Rachel took over. She told me she was not going to leave me here like this and either she was going to take me back to Atlanta, or help me find a place to live there.

I was so grateful she was there with me. I would not have been able to hold my sanity without her. Margaret did not want to get involved between two of her friends, so it was up to Rachel and myself to get me situated. According to Dave the landlord was only willing to give back half of our deposit, which he suggested he should keep for himself since I backed out on the deal. I said fine, anything to be done with it, but both Rachel and myself could not shake the feeling that I had just been taken for eight hundred dollars.

That night Rachel and I drove to Alexandria, Virginia just ten miles outside downtown DC. We got a hotel room because we needed to get away from Margaret's place to think of a plan. Rachel did most of the thinking because I was just to caught-up emotionally in what was going on. Nothing was working the way I'd planned. Rachel said she noticed a sign on a high-rise apartment building across the street that had apartments for rent, and she figured we would take a look there in the morning. That night she stayed up and prayed with me for strength and God's guidance for me, and she really made me feel like maybe things would be okay.

She was right, the next morning we went to that apartment building and rented a small studio efficiency apartment. It was only about five hundred square feet, but I felt safe. It was a good building, and my apartment was on the eleventh floor all the way at the end of the hall. Rachel cosigned with me to help me qualify for the apartment because I needed her longtime steady income on the application to quality. Even though I had a job with FedEx for five years, the last two while I was in Atlanta, I was only part-time.

Once that was done I felt a huge sense of relief. It was going to be about three days before I could move in, but that was okay with me as long as I had someplace. I felt relaxed so Rachel and I spent the next few days sightseeing together. We were really having a good time, and I was starting to worry that when Rachel left to go back home I was going to lose someone very special.

One afternoon while we were walking through the Mall by the Capitol building it started to downpour. The rain was coming down very hard in huge drops, but it felt good because it was so hot that day. Rachel and I started running through the park holding hands and laughing as we were getting soaked. We finally ran to the Smithsonian Nature Museum to get some shelter. We could not stop laughing, and as we stood there hugging on the grand steps on this huge building we kissed. It was one of those long passionate kisses, and I can say I was really feeling the love and caring for Rachel that I had worked so hard to repress. At that moment I couldn't help but think, "What was I going to do without this girl in my life"? I was having second thoughts about the idea of letting her go.

After a few days I got the building management's approval, Rachel helped me move into my new apartment. I had to report for work at FedEx the day I was allowed to move in, but Rachel helped unpack while I was at work. She basically set up most of my apartment for me.

After a few days Rachel was going to have to get back to Atlanta. As it was, she took off more than a week at her job to help me move in. I was not looking forward to her going. A small part of me just did not want to be left alone here, but a large part of me just did not want Rachel to not be a part of my life.

She had been there for me over the past year. She comforted me when I cried, and we shared good times too. Rachel helped me to heal and to feel love in my heart again. I could not let that go. My mind went back to a time just a few months earlier when Rachel and I went up to Nashville, Tennessee to visit her sister Brenda and see her new baby boy. The one sight I will never forget is Rachel rocking that baby in her arms while he slept peacefully on her chest. She would look up at me and smile as if to say, "This is the best life could ever be." I knew then Rachel would be a wonderful mother someday, and I started thinking that it was my children I wanted her to be the mother of.

When the day came for Rachel to leave we were sitting on the bed to say our goodbyes a few hours before her plane was set to take off. She looked at me and started to cry then she put her face in her hands. "I just don't want you to forget about me." She said.

"Rachel, sweetie, no, I could never forget about you...I love you." I said with tears in my eyes too.

With that she looked up, like those were the words she had been waiting to hear from me for a very long time. I think she knew I just didn't throw that phase around. For me to say it, I really meant it. She put her hands around my neck to hug me and said, "Oh. I love you too, I love you so much."

I kept kissing her cheek as she cried I could taste the tears on her cheeks. I could not lose her no way. I kept trying to assure her I was not going to leave her, which was a promise I had never made before to her, ever. I fell short however, of asking her to stay there with me. I felt guilty asking her to leave her job, and friends to move in with an emotionally and financially unstable guy like me.

That whole afternoon and at the airport we just kept saying, "I love you" to each other. It really felt good. For so long I kept my feelings for Rachel deep inside of me afraid to let them out, now here I was saying goodbye to her at the airport after I just moved seven hundred miles away like an idiot. When I was finally faced with the decision of either losing Rachel forever or advancing our relationship, I knew I had to take "us" to the next step.

We had a long passionate kiss at the gate to her plane and the last memory I had of Rachel is her mouthing, "I Love You" as she boarded the plane.

When she left I was a wreck. I could not believe I let her go. I cried the whole way back home. When I got there before I even went up to my apartment I called mom and dad from the parking garage payphone because my phone was not hooked up yet.

"Mom," I said with tears in my voice, "I just dropped off Rachel at the airport. I think I love her mom."

She was ecstatic, "I knew you would finally figure it out some-day, I just knew you loved her before you knew it. Oh honey, I'm so happy to hear you say that."

I told her I was going to ask Rachel to move to Washington with me, and mom thought that was a great idea. She was so happy. Mom loved Rachel a lot and knew she was the right one for me. My dad later got on the phone to tell me how happy he was too.

The very next day I called Rachel at her work to ask her if she would move up to Washington with me. She said, "You know, of course I will." I felt this was the best decision I had made in two years, and I was right. It was late June and Rachel said she had a few things to wrap up and she would be up by Labor Day. I felt on top of the world and in love, but it was about to be a very rough sum-mer.

CHAPTER 24

Once I knew Rachel was coming to be with me in a couple months I was feeling pretty good. I had made one of the best decisions I had ever made in my life up to that point, by not ending my relationship with her. I was feeling a sense of rightness, but at the same time a new sense of anxiety. As long as I never let my love for Rachel out, I felt I never had to worry about her safety or well-being. I wasn't worried about her being unfaithful or leaving me, but I was terribly frightened that what happened to Michelle could happen to her.

I had to know where she was and what she was doing all the time. There were times when I could not focus on what I was doing because I was always thinking about her and wondering whether she was safe or not. I felt totally helpless when Rachel was out of my sight, because I always wanted to be where I could protect her. I constantly gave her safety lectures on how to avoid being attacked, and how she must always be aware of what was around her. I guess Rachel felt I was over protective, but she fully understood why.

Working at FedEx was going fine. I didn't expect much out of it except a paycheck, so I wasn't disappointed. My heart wasn't really in it, and in my mind I was already done doing this kind of work. I felt it was my last tie to the way my life used to be, so I was looking forward to cutting it as quickly as possible. However, things would not go as smoothly as I planned.

My goals of working in Congress partly came to fruition within the first month. By mid-July I had a job working on the staff of a congressman from Upstate New York, but the hitch was I didn't get paid. I took the position on the staff because I hoped it would give me an "in" for paying jobs that would come up in other offices or committees later on. So, I worked at FedEx from six thirty a.m. to twelve p.m., and at the Capitol from one p.m. to 6 p.m. thru the month of July.

I would look for job openings and send out my resume everyday. I sent them by mail and delivered some of them in person, but I didn't have any success. It was much harder to get in than I thought for a few reasons, all of which weighed heavily against me. First of all, when the Republican Revolution took place a few months before, a lot of Democratic Party members were voted out of office leaving a large group of experienced former Capitol Hill staff people out of work. That left a huge pool of qualified people to fill very few available jobs. To make matters worse, most newly elected Republican congressmen brought their own staff with them. Had I been there in January when the new term started I may have had a better chance, but I was about six months too late.

The next big hurdle to over come was the budget battle that was brewing up between Congress and the President. That battle would lead to the "Big Government Shut Down of 1995" in the fall. So, that left most congressmen reluctant to hire anyone new because of course while they were trying on paper to make the government smaller, it just wasn't a good time to be making their personal staffs larger.

One of the biggest reasons however, was that I did not know the right people. The old saying, "Its not what you know, but who you know," goes double in Washington. Frankly, I don't even think the Congressman I worked for twenty hours a week knew my name or could pick me out of a lineup, so I got very little help there. I did not stop trying though.

The summer was moving along, I dropped into a comfortable schedule, and I still had a great deal of hope that I was going to eventually succeed. Then came the month of August which ranks up there to be probably the second most devastating periods in my life compared only to the time just after Michelle died.

I have a belief, that for me at least, when I am not quite on the path that God wants me to be on He kind of throws me off. With the rough move and all to Washington I did not quite get the same welcoming feeling and sense of relief I felt when I first got to Atlanta. However, I chose to just buckle down and keep my head focused on

my goals. God realized I did not get the message of what he was trying to tell me, so he had me take a time out by pulling me off my
schedule.

The first week of August my cousin Michael came down for what
was to be a weeklong visit. Michael is my Aunt Natalie's son who
was born on my thirteenth birthday and is more like a kid brother to
me than a cousin.

Within a couple days of his arrival I broke my right wrist, and
severely sprained my left wrist while playing softball with some of
my Capitol Hill co-workers. I was coming hard around third base
when the base, which was not anchored, slid out from under me and
I fell forward. I put my hands out in front of me to break my fall,
but instead I ended up breaking my wrist.

This was not good at all because I could not work at FedEx with
two injured wrists, and since I was only part-time I would not
receive any disability pay for the six weeks or so I was going to be
out. This was going to be a very difficult financial period for sure.

Two days after I broke my wrist, my grandmother Forte back in
Rochester died. Even though she had been sick for the past two
years or so I was devastated. Besides my own mother, my grandmother was the woman who was the biggest influence in my life
growing up. From the day I was born she had been there for me
helping to watch me in the evenings while my mother worked. She
was a strong disciplinarian, and was concerned that I stay on the
straight and narrow. My grandmother also showed me how much
she loved me with her undivided interest and attention.

My interest in politics also came from her. When President Carter
was running for office in 1976, I was probably the only kid in third
grade campaigning for the man at school because my grandmother
loved him so much.

She had always drummed in my head that graduating college was
one of the most important things I could do, and when I dropped out
of SUNY Buffalo I nearly broke her heart. After I finally graduated
from Georgia State I made a poster sized enlargement of my
diploma and gave it to her as a gift.

Grandma was also not very happy when I was marrying Michelle.
She thought that my blind love for her was what made me leave col-

lege. So, needless to say Grandma held a "you're ruining my grandson's life," grudge against her until just after our wedding. But, she did soften up very soon after.

When the weather was bad and I was working back in Rochester, Grandma would call my father worried about my safety. Dad would be direct with her, saying that she needed to leave me alone at work and that everything was fine. Then Grandma would call my home and talk with Michelle who always seemed to be able to put her at ease. She would say, "Grandma, Joey just called me to tell me he was doing okay. So, you have no need to worry." Michelle's demeanor was so sweet, and she made my Grandmother feel better every time they talked. So, the two of them started to develop a good relationship in the short time between our wedding and Michelle's death, and my grandmother was devastated when Michelle was murdered.

At the funeral she cried saying over and over "it should be me in that casket not Michelle, she was too young." Grandma often told me she would pray to Michelle to watch over us all, and she visited her grave sight every time she went to the cemetery to see my grandfather.

My family and I took Grandma's death very hard. The very next morning Michael and I made the seven-hour drive back to Rochester for the funeral. Since I couldn't work I planned on spending at least two weeks up there to be with my family.

Rachel took a flight in to be with me, which meant a lot to the whole family. Mom and Dad had just moved to Las Vegas a few months before, so we were all staying between my Aunt Natalie's house and my sister's.

This was going to be a horrible visit for me, everyone in the family including myself were out of sorts. We were all just beside ourselves with grief, and that seemed to make us pretty short with one another.

A few days after the funeral Rachel flew back to Atlanta, and Dad to Las Vegas, but Mom and I stayed for another week or so. It was during this time that I would experience what I believe to be a sign that would once again change my life and how I view my relationship with God forever.

I stayed in Rochester about two whole weeks total, and after the funeral was over I felt I had a few things I needed to do there before I made the trip back home. I don't really know why, but I needed to confront the devil on his turf in a matter of speaking. The fear I had for my safety was something I could deal with in Atlanta and Washington, but Rochester was still another matter.

I loved that city so much and all it meant to me growing up. The Italian community my family was a part of and its culture was not something I ever truly appreciated growing up, but I realized how much I missed it only after I left. Even with all the fond memories, I had only the horrible memories of Michelle's murder and the trial filled mind. For my emotional health I felt I needed to get back all the wonderful things I remembered from my days there.

Never once could I remember a positive memory about Michelle crossing my mind, in what was now over two and a half years since her murder. All I ever thought of when I thought of her was the night I found her or the guilt I still carried for being the one who was still alive. We had a great two years together, but I could not focus on the good times. Only the sight of her lifeless body covered in her own blood in the corner of our bedroom haunted me, at least once or twice everyday.

Memories of good times made me terribly depressed which was at times debilitating, but the hard times after her death filled me with rage toward Leroy and the evil he had done to the woman I loved. Frankly, for me anger was the emotion I was able to deal with much easier than depression. The anger helped to fuel me and give me the energy I needed to accomplish things, but the depression debilitated me and I would often get drunk to help me drown out my feelings.

One of the things I felt I needed to do was go to the scene of the murder again. I didn't feel I had to go into the duplex to complete this closure, but I needed to park outside where Michelle and I used to park and remember that night. When I pulled into the complex it was late afternoon, most of the people who lived there were not around. As soon as I saw the sign for Fleming Creek my heart started to pound almost out of my chest, but I drove in the parking lot anyway.

I parked there and looked up at the window that was our bedroom. It looked like there were new tenants living there, but they were not home. I know these people didn't know Michelle or myself, but I wonder how anyone could live there and be at peace with what had happened there. I wondered if Michelle's fear still lingered in that room, and could those who now slept there feel it. Was her spirit still there maybe waiting for me to come home?

I can't explain it but I felt a very uneasy and eerie feeling, like an evil presence was there in that apartment. That was what I needed to stand up to. I said out loud to myself, "You no longer have this power over me. That was a long time ago and I have beaten this." I stayed a little longer until I felt like the fear was replaced with confidence, then I left feeling I had done what I needed to do, by staring evil in the face and claiming my victory over it.

That night I would spend in my Aunt Natalie and Uncle Larry's house alone. They had left on a family vacation, which had been in the planning for months. Their house was only four or so miles from were Michelle and I used to live, and less than one mile from the police station where I had spent so many unpleasant hours. These thoughts came to mind a few times that day, but I really did not feel like it would be a problem for me.

However, when it came time for me to go to bed that night, it was a very different story. I was terrified, but I really did not understand why. I had been sleeping in my apartments by myself in Atlanta and Washington now for over a year with little or no fear at all, but now I felt like I did the night Rick and Michelle left me for the first time alone over two years ago.

I was so paranoid and afraid, I felt like a five-year-old. I must have gone down stairs to look out the windows every time a car drove by. I had every light in the place on and the TV all night. I basically passed out from exhaustion about two hours before the sun came up, and as soon as the sun did come up I was up for the day. It was a horrible night, and I did not do it again because I planned on spending the remainder of my Rochester stay at my sister and brother-in-law's house.

Before I went back though I wanted to go to the cemetery to pay another visit to the tombs of Michelle and my grandmother. After my Grandmother's funeral and we left her casket at the open entrance to her crypt, my entire family followed me to Michelle's tomb. This was the first time that Rachel would visit with me. I walked up to Michelle's nameplate and slowly rubbed my hand across it, and when I turned around more then twenty members of my extended family had been standing there behind me quietly just being there for me. In the front was Rachel who understood my past and was ready to walk with me into the future.

On this afternoon I went back to the cemetery, I needed to pay my respects alone, to talk with both of them, and to pray to God for direction. I had made a promise to Michelle that I would never let her die in vain, but that I would do something to make a difference for her sake. I wanted to let her know that I still felt that way, but I was at a loss as to what I should do and what direction I should follow.

As I sat on the bench in front on Michelle's tomb talking to her, there was a noise kind of like something sliding or being dragged across the floor of the mausoleum, but I was definitely the only person in the building. The sound was very close to me and echoed throughout the entire building. I was startled, but not afraid. It was like being touched by an old friend when you thought you were alone. It was pleasant, but my heart was still beating a mile a minute. I smiled and after a couple of minutes, I got up to look around. I was sure no one else was there except me. I started to approach the nameplate on Michelle's tomb, but I must admit I was a bit scared. I ran my hands slowly across her name then kissed the nameplate. When I turned around that was when I heard it.

The bells of the mausoleum started to play, "Ave Maria". Any other song or time would not have fazed me, but this was Ave Maria. Whenever I would go to visit her grave, I would hear Michelle singing that song in my head. The only positive memory I had of Michelle over the past two years was her singing that song with her mother. That song was able to break through my anger that prevented me from crying for so long. When I heard that song, I heard Michelle too.

I know this was no mere coincidence. I ran outside to look at the bell tower as the bells were ringing. The clock at the top of the tower said it was 4:38 in the afternoon, not the top of the hour or a fifteen minute fraction there of. I felt she and God had heard me. What that meant to me was that she heard me, and that she was around me. I now believe that she was happy for me, and the direction I was taking in my life, and that somehow she will always be there somewhere watching over my family and me. No one can tell me anything different. All my efforts were not going to waste because I am going to make it through all of this stronger than when I went into it. God was now calling me closer to Him.

CHAPTER 25

O nce I returned to Washington I entered into a very lonely and disturbing place. Even with the sense that Michelle was somehow pleased with my accomplishments I just could not seem to move on emotionally. All the things I had done since Michelle's death were only distractions so I wouldn't have time to feel the pain. Going back to college, and moving twice created only temporary excitement and direction, but as soon as the newness of these events wore off I was back to feeling without purpose once again.

Since the whole job seeking thing was a lot more difficult then I had imagined, and I seriously doubted my decision to move was the correct one. This time around I didn't hear the same voice of God telling me the next step he wanted me to take. I was lost. I felt God had left me out there to fend for myself, and I was dumb enough to not be within five hundred miles of anyone who could give me the love and understanding my family and close friends had.

I felt I screwed up bad. I was not in a good place emotionally. I wore the ink off those stupid tarot cards looking for answers, and flipped time and again through my Bible to try to find direction. I was frustrated, angry, depressed and the pain in my side that was caused by my stress and anger was getting unbearable. Because I was not working I would go days without interacting with any other people. I even tried searching the inter-net to find someone out there I could talk with. I felt if I expressed any of my deep-rooted feelings with anyone in my family all it would do was make them worry. Let's face it, I had geographically put myself in a difficult place to be reached.

I was scared and alone. I needed something, someone to give me direction. Someone to tell me there was a purpose to all I had gone through and a purpose to the life I was now leading. In absolute despair, and at the end of my rope emotionally after days of isolation, I finally dropped to my knees on my living room floor, and cried out to God for his direction. I was stretched out face down on the rug, grabbing onto the rug with both hands. I was in such despair I did not even feel the pain in my wrists that this position was causing me.

"God, what am I to do. I am tired of feeling these angry hurtful feelings, please Lord tell what I have to do."

Then came a voice like the one that had spoken to me which told me to leave for Atlanta... Not an audible voice. It was much louder than that... "Forgive."

"Forgive what? What do you mean," I said out loud.

"Forgive Leroy for what he has done." God replied back.

"Lord, no not that. I'll do anything else, but I can't forgive him I am sorry."

"You must forgive, for this is the only way you can be forgiven."

"Lord, I don't have it in me to forgive him. All I feel is hate for the man."

"You don't have to have the strength to do it on your own. You just need to say the words and I will help you, you see my Son's death on the cross was to cleanse the sins of the world and bring mankind closer to me. So, in Jesus' name if you ask for help to forgive Leroy, the Holy Spirit of God will help you."

So I began to pray, "Oh Lord I know I can't do this on my own, so I ask in the name of your son Jesus Christ to help me forgive Leroy. I forgive him for what he has done to Michelle. Lord please; forgive me for being so stubborn and holding on to my hatred. Please Jesus I invite you to come into my heart and fill this hole left by anger with your precious love. I dedicate my life to live for you Jesus, so just tell me where to go and I will go. I know I am a sinner, please forgive me for all my sins, cleanse me with the blood of your Son Jesus Christ."

Instantly I felt the peace of God come over me like a warm blanket. I felt his presence in me and with me like I hadn't felt before. The anger, hatred and pain in my side were gone. I realized God's intent, forgiving Leroy wasn't for Leroy at all. I am sure he could care less whether I forgive him or not, but my refusing to forgive was the only thing standing between me, and my relationship with God. This was what I was missing in my life. I needed to be working together with God and not against Him. At that very moment I had accepted Jesus Christ as my Lord and Savior, and my life would be different from that moment on.

I wish I could say every bit of ill feelings toward Leroy was completely gone, but I can say at least ninety percent of it was taken away from me right then and there on that living room floor. The pain in my side was gone and I felt like a weight had been lifted off of me.

Over the years since then I have had my brief moments of anger toward him only when I am reminded by similar murders that take place in the country, but I have learned in those times to focus on my Savior for strength at getting through those times. Christ Jesus loved us all and died for the sins of the world, so if Jesus loves me and I love Him, and Jesus loves Leroy then I must also love Leroy. I must admit that I don't fully understand it, but the good thing is that I don't have to, because God does.

I never again used the tarot cards after that moment on, or relied on psychics for advice and direction. I boxed up all that stuff and got rid of it for good. I realized the worst part of what I was doing was trying to mix God up with that whole mess. God had shown me that I was breaking his first commandment, "You shall have no other gods before me." and by searching for answers in that way was wrong, and I was putting the worst possible elements of darkness in front of God. You can't find God through "new age" ways, only evil can be found down that path.

I also now understand that you did not have to be worshiping another "god" or religion to be breaking this commandment, but anything you put before God as a priority to you breaks this commandment. That could be your love of money, your career, or even other people who work to distract you from your relationship with God. Jesus said, in Matthew 22:37-39 "You shall love the Lord your God with all your heart, and with all your soul, and with all your mind. This is the greatest and first commandment. And a second is like it: You shall love your neighbor as yourself. On these two commandments hang all the law and the prophets."

God never abandoned me. He was always there beckoning me, calling me to Him, saying as He did to Adam in the Garden, "Where are you?". However, my holding on to my anger toward Leroy and my reliance on new age mysticism only separated me from that true relationship with God that every human needs. The only way we can achieve that relationship is to admit to God we can't do it alone. We must ask Him to forgive us for our sins and accept Jesus Christ as our Lord and Savior, then He shall send His Holy Spirit to take up residence in your heart and seal you as one of His own. I was now radically changed forever, and not in a figurative way but in a literal way.

Christ changed my life permanently like none of the other outside adjustments I made could. Moving twice and going to school brought only temporary happiness, but God's forgiveness of me, and my forgiveness of Leroy brought a life change.

I had done what I had never thought I would do, and what I told Rachel I would never do. I let go of my hatred and I forgave the unforgivable act of murder. Now this does not mean I must forget what he did, or that I feel Leroy should be freed from jail. God does not expect that, nor will me ever ask it of His people. These are the Lord's Commandments and the law of the land that we shall not murder. Now God's relationship with Leroy is between the two of them, and I am not involved in that.

All God wanted me to do was lay all those hateful feelings at the foot of the cross where His son was crucified. It was not very difficult to forgive others when I stopped to think of all God had forgiven me for, and the sacrifice his Son had made for me on that cross at Calvary.

My life from that moment on had changed forever, and I didn't have to go up to where God was, because He came down to me because He loves me.

If God loves me so much then how could He have let this happen to Michelle? I honestly don't know, but what I do know is that the Bible is full of good God fearing men and women who had suffered even more tragic events than I had. Through it all though, they kept their faith in God and in return God greatly blessed them.

God never promised us that we would lead a life free of sorrow, but He did promise that He would be our comforter and that all things shall work toward the glory of God. He gave us all a free will, which is truly the only way we can really love Him. If He somehow did not give us a free will or a mind to decide for ourselves then how can there be true love. Because love is something that is given freely and true love can never be forced.

However, because we have free will and all the benefits that come with it, some will use it for hate and there is very little we can do about it. I believe God, the creator of the Universe could have stopped Michelle from being killed if that was His plan, but for some reason that my earthly mind can't understand He didn't. Maybe it was His plan that through her life and her death, that others would be drawn closer to Him and just maybe the testimony of Michelle's life could somehow make a difference to someone who was in despair. Anyway, whatever it was that God had in mind I was letting Him know that I was on board and willing to do my part in serving Him.

I was now freed from the burden of an unforgiving heart and I was grateful to God for that. He changed my life and in the process saved it too. Christ took away my pain and allowed me to heal, and from that moment on my life would not be the same. He helped me to deal with my grief and opened my heart giving me the ability to love and be loved.

Sure, there have been brief moments of pain in my life since, and a red carpet has not been laid out before me. Christ did not promise me a perfect problem free life. However, the depths of my depressions are one tenth as deep as they were, and the darkness contains a light that gives me hope.

I have been able to move on with my life and put that terrifying event behind me while keeping the lessons God has taught me through this in front of me to light my path as I have moved through life. A person much wiser than I once said, we can never experience true happiness unless we have experienced great sorrow. I have learned never to take the simple blessings in life for grated, but to experience life with love, joy and hope.

CHAPTER 26

Rachel came to Washington two weeks after that life altering decision in mid September. Two weeks before Christmas that year I asked her to be my wife. I felt that that was what God had intended from the very beginning of our relationship and I knew in my heart that I wanted to spend the rest of my life with her.

I must say I think I did a much better job this time proposing to her than I had done with Michelle, perhaps I had learned from my previous mistakes. I took Rachel to our favorite Italian restaurant IL' Porto in Old Town Alexandria, Virginia. I made sure to tell them at the restaurant that I was planning a proposal that night. I had two different plans. I was first going to test the water at dinner and ask Rachel if she wanted to take a walk along the boardwalk after we ate. If she were to say "no, it was too cold", then I would pop the question during dessert. If she said "yes", I wanted to take her by the Potomac River to propose on the boardwalk.

When I asked her, she said she would really enjoy a walk, so I had my answer. However, I failed to mention my whole plan to the staff at the restaurant. They only knew that I was going to propose, so they kept staring at our table waiting to see when I going to do it. When the waiter would come to the table he would give me the old head nod and raised eyebrow look. When Rachel left to go to the restroom the waiter came up to ask if I had done it yet, and what did she say. I filled him in on my plan, and although he seemed a bit disappointed he said that was an excellent and romantic idea.

After a wonderful romantic dinner we took a stroll along the boardwalk. It is a beautiful scene there that night with the moon reflecting off the water, and the Washington monument and Capital building visible far off across the Potomac River.

I sat her down on a bench and got on one knee. "Rachel, I love you so much, and I would be honored if you would spend the rest of your life with me as my wife."

She looked at me and smiled, "Of course, you know I will."

I reached in my pocket, and said, "Well then, I guess you will be needing this." I had a ring custom made for her at a jewelry store there in Alexandria. She was very surprised. I think she expected that sooner or later I would propose, but I know she did not think she would be getting an engagement ring.

Sometime later she told me that on that day in my apartment in Washington just before she was going to leave for Atlanta that she had talked to Michelle. Rachel told her that she knew Michelle loved me, but that if she would let go that she would be sure to take good care of me.

On October 12, 1996 Rachel and I were married back in Rochester. It was a great celebration, and I felt so much love and joy from my family who for the past three and a half years had been there for me in my grief.

Two months after our wedding Rachel and I moved back to Atlanta. We felt that Washington was really not the place where we were meant to be, but God had His purpose for me fulfilled in the time we had spent there.

On March 26, 1998 we would celebrate the birth of our first daughter Marilyn Rosalie, named after both Rachel's mother and mine. At that very moment as I held our child in my arms, I felt like my life had come full circle. God had truly blessed my life beyond what I could have ever hoped for five years before. On August 3, 2000 our second daughter Katherine "Katie" Marie was born. The love that I feel for my children is unmatched by anything I have ever experienced in my life. They are truly my joy.

God has continued to do a work in my life as a Christian and He continues to draw me into closer fellowship with Him. I feel free and I believe I am a better husband and father than I may have been because of my experiences. I love life and view it as a blessing from God, and I truly appreciate my family.

I also have a clearer idea of what it means to be a success in life. For a long while I felt that I needed to have some powerful government job that I felt would give me the opportunity to change the world and make it a better place to live. Although that can be important, God calls each of us to be living testaments of His grace and love for us. This way we can have a real impact on those we come into contact along life's journey.

A short time after my oldest daughter was born I had a dream just as I was drifting off to sleep one night. In this dream I woke up in the bed Michelle and I shared in our townhouse back in Rochester. It was morning and the sun lit up the room, and as I sat up Michelle was lying next to me with the smile that always warmed my heart. "Good Morning, sweetie." she said.

The strangest thing was that in my dream I had remembered all that had happened, with Michelle being murdered, and everything that had transpired in my life since then. But, it felt so real; somehow I was back at that time in my life again.

What was I doing there I thought. Could everything before this been a dream? I jumped out of bed and ran to the dresser where I kept my wallet and opened it up. Right there in the front was a picture of my daughter in the place I kept it. There was also a picture of Rachel and I together in there as well.

I was confused and although I was in a familiar place without any fear, I knew this wasn't where I was supposed to be. "Michelle," I said, "I cannot stay here with you. I have moved on, my family needs me."

Michelle looked up at me smiling and said, "I know, I have just been waiting to hear you say it. All I ask is that you never forget me and the hardship God has carried you through, and don't forget that I will always love you."

CPSIA information can be obtained
at www.ICGtesting.com
Printed in the USA
BVHW071419120620
581230BV00004B/127

9 781591 606239